Tahira The Elemental

Derek M Cartwright

Published by Quite Good Books, 2024.

This is a work of fiction. Similarities to real people, places, or events are entirely coincidental.

TAHIRA THE ELEMENTAL

First edition. October 14, 2024.

Copyright © 2024 Derek M Cartwright.

ISBN: 978-1917495011

Written by Derek M Cartwright.

Author's Note

• • • •

Since the birth of our species we humans have told each other stories. Tales of great heroes and leaders who defied the odds to overcome various forces of evil.

Over time these have become myths and legends with each civilisation having it's own sagas about the 'ancient ones'.

As each millennia progresses these chronicles become more embellished and more fantastic. Any supporting archeaological evidence has been lost over time so all we have are these stories and, they can't possibly be true, can they?

DEREK M CARTWRIGHT

Europia

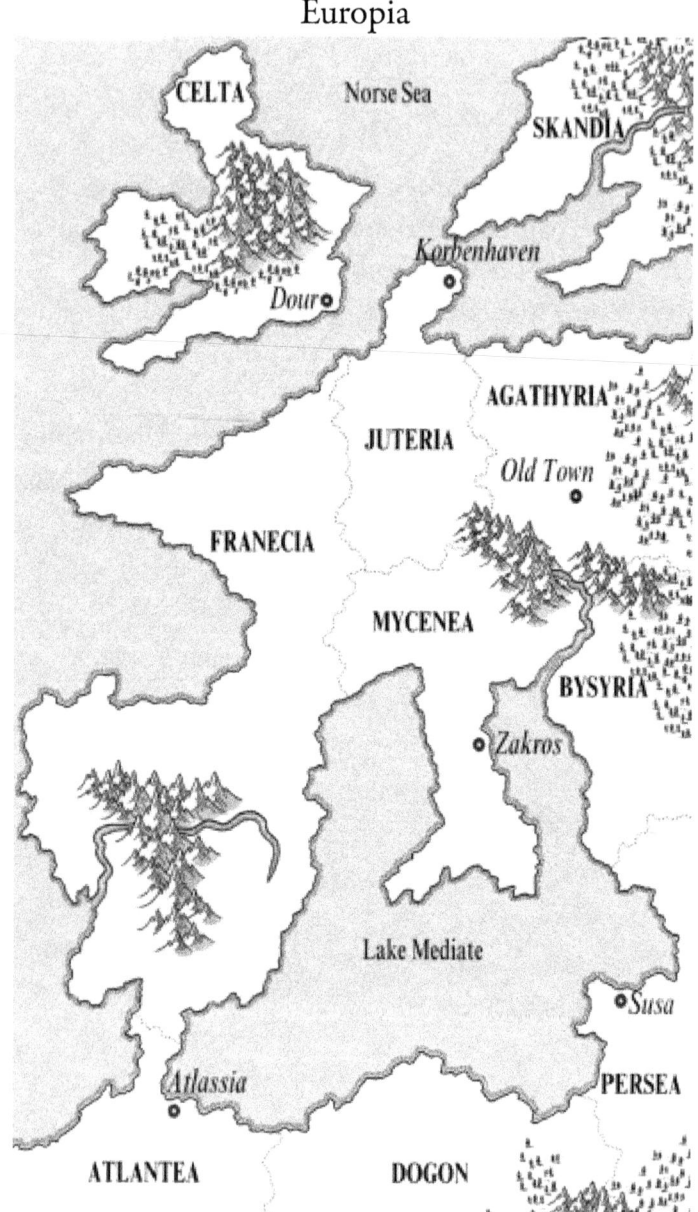

TAHIRA THE ELEMENTAL

Name	Meaning
Matai	(matt-ay) A Gift from God (org: Hebrew)
Tahira	(ta-here-rah) Pure and Virtuous (org: Arabic)
Koranda	(core-and-a) Good Fortune and Health (org: Sanskrit)
Potolo	(pot-oh-low) The Smallest Star (org: Dogon)
Siria	(sy-rea) Glowing and Sun-Bright (org: Persian)
Kadidia	(cad-id-ee-a) The Precious One (org: Mali)
Dogon	(doh-gone) A Pagan Stranger (org: Habbe – early Mali)
Adama	(adam-r) Earth (org: Hebrew)
Adeveima	(add-eve-ema) Life (org: Latin – derived from the name Eva)
Yurugobi	(you-ru-go-bee) Relaxed and calm (org: Japanese)
Atalasian	(at-alas-eon) Enduring (org: derived from Greek Titan)
Felix	(fee-licks) Happy or Lucky (org: Latin)
Amir	(am-ear) Prince (org: Arabic)
Lucretus	(loo-cre-tuss) Wealth (org: derived from similar Latin name)
Elita	(ee-leet-ah) Chosen One (org: Latin)
Amastan	(am-a-stan) Protector (org: early Amazigh)
Kahina	(ca-heen-a) A Sorceress (org: Arabic)
Lunja	(lun-yah) Fairytale Princess (org: Berbers)
Jamilah	(ja-mill-lar) Beautiful (org: Arabic)
Chike	(che-kay) Talented (org: ancient Egypt)
Abidemi	(ab-ee-dem-ee) Born during father's absence (org: Yoruba)
Alba	(al-bah) A Noble, Shining One (org: Germanic)

DEREK M CARTWRIGHT

Name	Meaning
Sadiri	(sah-diree) One who is Powerful (org: N. African poss. Berber)
Makida	(ma-key-dah) Sweetness or Honey (org: Ethiopean)
Zawahi	(sah-wa-hee) Quick minded (org: Arabic)
Airyaman	(air-ee-man) God of Health and Healing (org: Zoroastrian)
Tudiya	(tu-dee-ah) The 1st Assyrian King (org: Assyria)
Thriti	(three-tee) Happiness (org: Hindu)
Tudizade	(tu-dee-zar-dee) Tudiya's son (org: Arabic)
Jasmina	(jazz-mean-a) A Gift from God (org: Persian)
Olenus	(ol-en-us) Mythological creature (org:
Namud	(nah-mood) Worthy of Admiration (org: Persian)
Morgana	(moor-gan-a) Enchantress (org: Welsh Celtic)
Astra	(a-strah) From the Stars (org: Greek)
Nawali	(na-wah-lee) Kindness and Charity (org: Arabic)
Sigurd	(see-gourd) Guardian of Victory (org: Norse)
Gustav	(gus-taff) Royal staff (org: Norse)
Sigurdsson	(see-gourd-son) Son of Sigurd (org: Norse)
Zirak	(zee-rack) Intelligent (org: Persian)
Seren	(sa-wren) Star (org: Welsh Celtic)

Firestarter

"Tahira, wake up, it's time." Matai gently shook Tahira's shoulder to rouse her from her fitful sleep. Tahira nodded as she opened her bleary eyes. The two women quickly and silently left the female sleeping quarters. The other slaves did not need to be woken.

Matai was tall and slender with skin the colour of night. She was a strong and powerful woman. Rumour was that she came from a warrior tribe in a land faraway. Approaching her thirtieth year she was older than the others and had quickly risen to be the head of the slaves.

Matai was also Lord Koranda's favourite concubine and as such enjoyed a level of freedom not bestowed to the other captives. She had never viewed it as anything other than a strategy for survival.

They entered the room where Tahira's father lay dying. The cancer had robbed Potolo of his handsome features. As he entered the last hour of his life it had also dulled the sparkle in his eyes. Tahira rushed to him and held him as a single tear slowly descended from her strikingly beautiful emerald green eyes, caressing her fair youthful skin. It glistened in the first rays of sunlight, shining like a tiny pear cut diamond.

Smiling, Potolo carefully wiped away her tear before stroking her long, dark auburn hair, "Now, now, my dear Tahira." Potolo's once commanding voice was now merely a breathless whisper. He coughed as he fought for air. "Rest assured I am going to a better place, your mother is already waiting for me." Once more he paused, once more he coughed.

"Here take this. Your mother made me promise on her deathbed to give you this on your sixteenth birthday. I am happy to have survived just long enough to fulfil her wish." He handed his daughter a soft leather pouch.

"It is beautiful Father." Tahira viewed the small round amulet with a mix of sadness and awe. It was no more than two inches in diameter and divided into four quarters. Each of which had a flat, clear quartz crystal expertly encased in a silver band. Whilst looking at this talisman Tahira regretted that she had never known her birth mother. How could she? She had died during childbirth. Her father had often spoken about his wife Siria, and about his complete and utter love for her. Tahira knew that he felt the pain of her loss every single day. He would say that he was blessed to have known her love and cursed to have lost it.

"Not in comparison to you my darling daughter." Potolo's wheezy voice broke her train of thought, "I have held this everyday as a reminder of your mother. I had a leather strap made so you can wear it around your neck." He gestured for Tahira to put it on. His breath weakened, "So beautiful just like your mother." He whispered. Smiling once more, he closed his eyes.

They knew this day was coming. Potolo was the last of the male slaves. Although he had lived all his life in the cold, wet northerly lands of Celta he had a gift for languages. The foreign people he had met along the way had been more than willing to share their knowledge. It was this ability that had kept him alive for so long. Lord Koranda had used him well and saw him as an asset. Koranda also knew that because he held his

TAHIRA THE ELEMENTAL

daughter that Potolo would never try to escape for fear of what Lord Koranda would do to her if he did.

The other half dozen slaves helped bury Potolo and wished his spirit well on its journey to the afterlife. No more tears were shed and soon everyone resumed their daily duties. Any act deemed to upset their overlords would only lead to a severe beating or worse.

Tahira kept her birthday gift well hidden. Her duties were light, mainly because Matai had warned the other female slaves to show some respect for Tahira's bereavement. During the afternoon Matai was summoned to speak with Lord Koranda, She returned thoughtful and distant. Whilst everyone else prepared and served the evening meal Matai took Tahira to the bathing room. Matai added a few herbs and spices to the warm water in the large copper bowl. Without any exchange of words Matai washed Tahira's hair. She stood back admiring her handiwork. Matai said, "There you go, my pretty Princess, let's take you to see our master."

Tahira felt a wave of panic come over her. Why would Lord Koranda want to speak with her? Matai waved away her concerns although it did little to ease her mind.

As they reached Lord Koranda's sleeping quarters Matai offered Tahira a small vial of liquid. "Take it, it will help, it will also prevent any accidents."

Tahira shook her head. The door opened and she entered. Matai quickly retreated, to her own quarters, with tears streaming down her face.

"Ah Tahira, do come in." Lord Koranda allowed his eyes to take in the full splendour of the young woman before him. He approached Tahira who was rooted to the spot. He lifted her long hair to his nostrils and savoured the heady scent. "I am sorry to hear about your father, he was a man of many talents and was very useful to me. I shall miss him." He moved to stand behind Tahira and placed his hands on her shoulders. "You are such a beautiful young woman." He kissed her exposed neck. She recoiled involuntarily and turned to face her overlord. He cared not. Reaching for the top of her dress with both hands he ripped it apart revealing her breasts. She stepped away, doing her best to maintain her modesty. She began to cry.

"Oh you are a spirited one. I like that. I shall enjoy this all the more." He took a step towards her.

"*Burn!*" Tahira didn't hear the word nor did she say the word. It was as if she 'felt' the word as a whisper lost on a breeze.

"You will do what I say, I am your lord and master." He shouted before slapping her across the face with the back of his hand. She stumbled backwards against his bed.

"*Burn!*" It came to her again. She sensed it grow louder. It was a thought but it was gaining in intensity as her anger grew.

Once more he hit her before throwing her on his bed. He lay on top of her, grunting like a pig.

He grabbed her jaw to make her look at him. He tried to kiss her. Tahira didn't want to look at this odious man. She tried to turn her face away. But he was far stronger than her. She felt the anger well inside her. But she didn't scream, she didn't shout. Her inner voice told her to wait. Then she felt her body relax. She had the sensation of leaving her body.

Lord Koranda smiled, he had broken her will. He now stood up in front her and began to undo his belt. As he did so he reached down and began to lift Tahira's skirt exposing her thighs.

And now the anger returned. This time there was no rebuke, this time there was no control, as she felt the anger feed on itself. Her rage deepened and intensified, she felt it would explode from within her body.

"*Burn!*" The inner voice shouted.

Tahira was no longer aware of what was happening to her. She was separated from herself and her surroundings.

"*BURN!*" The howling scream came from Tahira. Her fury and her grief had compelled it forth. Her world became black. Tahira passed out.

• • • •

"Here, have some water!" Matai's familiar voice reassured Tahira. Resting on her elbow she did as she was commanded. Through tired eyes she surveyed her surroundings not understanding where she was or how she got here. She did however feel safe. She felt the bruise on her jaw and the horror of her memory came flooding back. She closed her eyes and lay back down on the grass hoping she had had a nightmare and that everything would be OK when she woke up.

Matai ignored Tahira's discomfort. "We don't have that much time for you to have another nap." There was an element of playfulness in her words but, Tahira knew her well enough not to play dead for long.

"I have so many questions." Tahira had managed to get herself into a sitting position. She looked down at her clothes, "But first, why are we dressed as men?"

Matai smiled as she expertly pulled herself up into the saddle of a large black mare. "Male travellers don't get as much grief as female ones. Come on we need to get out of here!"

Tahira knew instinctively not to argue and quickly mounted the companion steed, she waved a finger in Matai's direction, "That looks like Lord Koranda's horse and mine looks like his son's."

"You are very observant my little firestarter." Tahira recoiled with horror at the memory triggered by Matai's words. Ignorant of how Tahira was feeling Matai turned to point a finger, "Look," Tahira's eye's followed the direction indicated, "That is what's left of Lord Koranda's place."

From their hilltop vantage point they could easily see the smouldering smoky remnants of what had been a large fortified homestead. The main feasting hall had been burned to the ground as had the adjoining rooms of the master and his extended family. Even the roofs on the slave's roundhouses had succumbed to what was a ferocious wildfire. Stables and animal pens had gone up in smoke too. The only things still standing were a few stone walls along with the enclosure bank and ditch.

With a deft tug on the hemp rope reins Matai turned the horse's head away from the charred ruins and began to walk slowly along an old trading route heading south. Tahira's horse naturally followed the head mare and pulled up alongside.

"But I didn't do anything, he attacked me and I passed out, thankfully!"

"Look," Matai was calm and controlled but did not return her gaze, "I don't know who or what, you are but I know what I saw." If she expected Tahira to interrupt she was sadly mistaken, she carried on. "You see, I knew what he was going to do to you and I couldn't bear it so I went back to my bed chamber and grabbed my knife. Before he touched you I was going to stab him in the back and you and I were going to have to try and escape. I could hear his familiar grunting so I peeped through the gap in the door frame to see him standing in front of you with his trousers round his ankles. I knew that was the time I had to strike so I silently began to open the bed chamber door and saw an ethereal image of you standing beside the bed detached from your body which was lying on the bed. I was frozen to the spot as you reached out with your arms and a blinding white light came forth. You touched Koranda and he began to burn outwards from that point. He screamed in agony as his body collapsed into white hot ash. You then turned around and everything that the white light touched began to burn ferociously hot. The heat was intense and I lost sight of you so I ran. The flames spread quickly and I only just made it in time to free the other slaves. I opened the stables and animal pens and we all ran as fast as our legs would take us."

Tahira simply shook her head. She knew that in her anger she had thought the word 'burn' but, what Matai had described just wasn't possible!

Unaware of Tahira's internal dialogue, Matai continued, "Once I made it to the woods I stopped to grab my breath and looked back. The homestead was engulfed but the fire was contained within. I watched throughout the night as the flames dimmed. At first light I went back to see if there was anything left that I could make use of, and there you were, fast asleep surrounded by piles of ash. I couldn't wake you so I brought you outside and carried you up to the hill and that was a couple of days ago."

"Well I am grateful to you for looking out for me and, I am sorry too." Tahira didn't know what else to say.

Matai shrugged her shoulders as she interrupted, "There is absolutely no need to apologise. I was not going to let that bastard take you the way he had taken me." She paused briefly, "You see we had a deal. I would give myself to him willingly, as long as, he didn't touch you or the other girls." She took a quick breath before she hissed, "My only regret is that it wasn't my knife that killed him."

"But, it wasn't me, honest, I don't know who you saw but I am not some sort of witch." Tahira protested her innocence even though she knew deep down, that she had caused something to happen. She had lost control and she didn't like it.

"There are a lot of things that go on in this world that I do not understand, but, I know what I saw. Now, if you are telling me that you are not a witch then you are not a witch I don't really care, but." She paused thoughtfully, "The thing is, as I said before, I was going to kill him anyway so you saved me the trouble but."

"Can you stop saying but all the time?" Tahira smiled.

Matai returned the gesture.

"Also," Tahira continued, "I think we are being followed, two men, up on the ridge about two hundred yards away."

Matai cursed, she should have spotted them herself. Still no matter, she pushed her horse into a gallop. Tahira's quickly followed. After a few hundred metres Matai pointed the horses towards a small copse.

There would-be assailants followed suit. In the thicker part of the bush they were forced to dismount. This was the last mistake they made. Tahira acted as a decoy. Whilst their attackers were distracted, Matai threw a knife into the back of the skull of one of them. He was dead before he hit the ground. The other turned and ran towards Matai with his sword raised. He didn't get within ten paces before he too felt the fatal sensation of a cold metal knife puncture his skull. They quickly and dispassionately took whatever they could reuse or sell on before hiding their naked bodies in the undergrowth.

Matai checked over the bandit's horses and decided that they could trade them in later. With longer leads she attached one horse to each of their own horse's reins. Picking up the trackway they continued their journey.

"Friends of yours were they?" Tahira's voice was dripping with sarcasm.

"Well, they were last night, after making sure you were safe I came back down to the enclosure and they saw me. I could see from the look in their eyes that robbing me was not the only thing they wanted so, I still had that vial I offered you so I took it. I learned a long time ago that sex can be a very powerful weapon and I have been known to use it to my advantage from time to time. When it was over they promptly fell asleep so I tied them up and took their spare clothes, and what little money they had on them." Matai waved a finger in Tahira's direction, "I don't think they were coming to have a nice little chat with me, do you? Oh, I gave you the shorter man's clothes."

Tahira sarcastically sniffed her shirt, "And the smelliest ones as well." She looked at Matai thoughtfully, "So do you have a plan? Are we going anywhere in particular?" she asked.

"We are heading towards the Port of Dour on the South Coast. However, I, not we," Matai was quite determined, "will then seek a safe passage across the sea and begin the long journey back to my homeland. I have had enough of your long cold nights in the winter and the incessant rain. I want to go back some place warm where I don't have to wear three layers of clothes just to stop shivering. You are of course free to go home, wherever that is."

"But I don't have a home, well not anymore and I have no family, my father was the only family I knew, he always said that we were descended from the Beaker people but born to be nomads," Tahira's voice was reflective, "Can I not come with you, at least part of the way?"

"I do not need a burden. My journey is long and dangerous." As Matai looked into her young friend's eyes her tone softened slightly, "However, your, let's call them unique abilities, might be useful." She sighed, "OK young lady, what say you? I let you tag along and, I will teach you how to be a warrior while you help me with finding food?"

Tahira quickly nodded her understanding and acceptance. She desperately wanted to talk about her experience but how could she explain it if she couldn't understand it herself. They carried on in silence until nightfall when they pitched camp in a small wood. They were now physically and mentally miles away from their former lives as slaves.

Matai took first watch.

Just before she closed her eyes Tahira gazed at the brightest star in the night sky. Was it her imagination or was there a new companion star next to it? Silently saying goodnight to her mother and father she drifted off into a restless sleep.

The Road to Dour

As the first rays of sunlight broke through the dawn mist Tahira woke. She smiled to herself as she gazed upon Matai asleep propped against a rock. Their camp fire had long gone out. As she edged closer to wake her friend she was startled to see Matai instantly wake up and grab her throwing knife.

"You make too much noise!" Matai admonished.

"And you are definitely not a morning person." Tahira rose quickly and went off to search for some fresh pine needles to make their morning tea. "You should have woken me to take my turn at being on watch. Oh and you let the fire go out!"

Their meagre breakfast did not take long to consume. "So let's begin your training." Matai rose and beckoned Tahira to stand in front of her. She then proceeded to go through a series of muscle stretches and exercises commanding Tahira to repeat. She scolded her when she made a mistake and Tahira quickly learnt that Matai was not going to be an easy taskmaster.

By the time Matai ordered an end to the exercises Tahira was red in the face and short of breath.

"Right," Matai didn't allow Tahira to rest for long, "I want you to attack me and I will defend myself."

As inexperienced as Tahira was this was not something she enjoyed. Every lunge, every feint was met with a snort of derision and a kick up the backside.

"You fight like a little girl," Matai chided, "I want you to fight like a man."

There was a twinkle in Tahira's eye as she stopped and audibly broke wind, "Like that you mean!" Matai laughed.

Seeing an opportunity Tahira aimed a sweeping kick towards Matai's left ankle, successfully causing Matai to lose her balance and fall to the ground. Tahira pounced but Matai had quickly regained her composure planting her foot firmly in Tahira's stomach and rolling her off to one side. Tahira knew what was coming next and she felt yet another leather encased foot connect with her butt cheeks.

"Inventive." Matai smiled as she hauled Tahira back onto her feet. "That's enough for now."

Breaking camp they continued their journey.

"That's such a pretty necklace." Matai pointed to the amulet around Tahira's neck. "What stone is that red one?"

Confused Tahira took off her jewel and was astonished to see one of the quarters was now blood red. She stuttered her reply, "I don't know, I thought it was the same as the other three but clearly my mind has been playing tricks on me, as you saw, my father gave it to me on his deathbed, and I really have no other information about it." She rehung it around her neck, it felt warm and reassuring.

They rode in silence for several hours stopping occasionally to rest their horses and forage for food. As dusk fell they settled by the campfire to eat.

"So how did you end up as one of Lord Koranda's slaves?"

If Matai was shocked at the impertinence of Tahira's question she didn't show it. She simply carried on sipping her tea before she casually responded, "My father sold me."

Tahira's jaw hit the floor. Matai inwardly smiled, she had not told this story before and she savoured the shock her statement had instilled in her young friend. But still she hesitated, not from any potential mistrust of her ward but of the pain the memory invoked.

Matai took a deep breath, "From a very young age, about five or six I think, I had been promised to a man from a neighbouring tribe. He was several years older than me. It was agreed that the day of my sixteenth birthday was to be the date for our 'joining'. Over the preceding years we would spend time together. I think both families hoped we would grow to love each other but the age difference was too great. He constantly teased me and belittled me. When no one was looking he would beat me much like my older brothers did. Left alone one night when I was thirteen he raped me. When I told my Mother she was distraught and tried to get him punished but my Father ignored her wishes and insisted the marriage would go ahead as planned."

Tahira now understood the 'bond' between her and Matai. She had gone through this herself. She wanted to ask questions, she wanted to offer support to console but, something inside her told her that the best thing to do was to listen.

The pain was beginning to rise in Matai but she also felt herself somewhat removed. It surprised her how cold she had become. She was recounting something personal to her and although there was grief and rage it was detached as if she was telling a tale about someone else.

She continued, "Unknown to my Father, my Mother took me to a local medicine woman who gave me a vial of liquid to drink. This made me as sick as a dog but she told me it would stop me from bearing fruit. She then gave me a recipe that would send me into the 'dream world' if I had to go to him again. This is the one I prepared for you the other day."

Tahira nodded her understanding.

Darkness had now descended and the amber glow from the firelight and the crackle from the firewood broke Matai's spell. "Anyway," Matai paused briefly, "that's enough reminiscing for now. It was a long time ago and you need to get some rest. I'll take first watch."

Yawning Tahira replied, "You know that I will want to hear more, if there is anything that I can do to help?"

Matai smiled, "Oh don't worry, you have already done that my friend!"

"Tahira, Tahira, can you hear me? Can you feel me?"

It was no more than a whisper. Tahira tried to open her eyes but couldn't, nor could she move her mouth to respond. She suddenly realised it was another of her weird, lucid dreams. It had been a while but somehow this one seemed stronger, more forceful. She mentally projected a greeting.

"Oh good, at long last, I have waited so long,"

Tahira felt the happiness and sheer joy from her communicator. There was warmth in that inner voice, it was ethereal but she felt, love.

"There isn't much time but you need to wake up now and wake your friend and hide further in the forest, go now, quickly!"

Tahira suddenly woke, aware that she was holding her amulet she quickly and quietly moved towards Matai. As she placed her hand over Matai's mouth Matai woke up. Looking into Tahira's eyes and without saying a word they quickly killed the fire and moved further into the forest. Once Tahira felt that they would be safe they stopped. Dawn was beginning to break through. Matai turned to her young companion and was just about to challenge her when she heard what first appeared to be a low rumble. Their horses heard it too and they began to get agitated. Tahira and Matai worked to keep their steeds calm as the rumble grew into a thunderous roar. In the dim light they could see the galloping rabble of men and the wagon they were escorting careering within fifty paces of their camp. They didn't need to look twice, they knew they were slavers. Another cargo of human traffic destined for a life of servitude. If they hadn't hidden they would have been added to the list.

They remained silent as the sound of the horses' hooves diminished. As the bird song returned Matai once more took charge and mounted her horse and set off with Tahira by her side.

"So, are you going to tell me?" Matai was concerned, not just about how fortunate they had been but also how she hadn't woken when Tahira had moved. She was so practiced in her ability to sleep lightly and to wake at the slightest sound that she was shocked to think that Tahira could be so deftly quiet especially as she had moved as loud as a bone flute not twenty four hours ago.

"Not sure really, I," Tahira hesitated, "I woke up thinking it was my turn to keep watch," she was uncomfortable with the lie but, as she couldn't explain it herself, she simply went with it, "and I could hear something in the distance and, panicked I suppose."

Matai knew there was more to this than she had been told but the quizzical look on Tahira's face convinced her to leave it alone, for now.

They carried on with their slow pace until they came to a ford on a river. At this point Matai ordered that they now follow the river and not the roadway as it would be safer.

Without waiting for the question, Matai offered the fact that all rivers in this part of the kingdom flowed south. By following the river they would eventually end up on the coast and hopefully, at a trading port, they could buy a boat ride to freedom and home.

After travelling for three or so leagues Matai indicated that they should make camp. After a quick search she found a small rocky outcrop within the heavily wooded area. "Right," she said, "this will be as good a place as any to stay for a few days, I want to concentrate on your training."

Tahira smiled although this was as much through trepidation as anything else. With their backs against the cliff face they made a temporary shelter which offered a nice wide view down the slight slope to the river. Before they settled in for their evening meal they took the opportunity to bathe and wash their clothes.

"Do you miss your mother and father?" an emboldened Tahira asked after they had eaten.

"Oh I miss my mother sometimes, her name was Kadidia," Matai waited for the pain and anger to rise in her veins but there was nothing. Her voice became cold, "But my father, no, I would never give him that, satisfaction!" Once more she paused, she couldn't remember the last time she had spoken about her family and her past and yet here she was reminiscing, if that was the right word for it, with a girl nearly half her age, "My father was Dogon, he was the leader of our tribe. There were many in my clan that felt he was a good leader, a strong and powerful one. After defeating the neighbouring tribe and killing their leader Adama, he took Adama's wife, Adeveima, to be his second wife. This was not uncommon for my people. My

Mother retained her position as first wife but to do so she had to agree to the joining together of the two tribes. This is why my marriage was proposed. I was to wed Yurugobi, the eldest son of Adeveima."

"So Yurugobi is the one who attacked you?"

Matai nodded, "Yes and he asked for me several more times once I entered womanhood. I took my drink and did my tribal duty but my hatred for Yurugobi, his family and my father grew each time. I secretly began to practice hunting and other warrior skills. Through training and exercise I became more proficient. Over the next couple of years my confidence grew but I never displayed my skills. Even my mother never knew. As I grew stronger and fitter so sadly her health declined. After a few months my father preferred the company of his second wife. I believe my mother was slowly poisoned by Adeveima, she died a few years later when I was fifteen or so."

At this point Tahira noticed a slight brightening in Matai's face but didn't get a chance to comment.

Matai was now having happier thoughts. "After my mum's funeral I went off into the bush to be alone with my thoughts and there I met Atalasian. He was from another village and was performing his Sigue initiation. It's a series of tests that boys do in order to become men. He was tall and handsome but a useless hunter. He couldn't go back until he had caught something and the bigger, stronger and more ferocious the animal the better. He made me laugh as we camped out under the stars and told each other tales of our ancestors. I took him and it was glorious. In the morning we tracked and killed a desert lion. I watched as he dragged the beast back to his village. I could hear their shouts and whistles. I know he looked back for me but I was hidden. Look I kept a claw as a reminder of our time together." Matai briefly revealed her own necklace before continuing, "Although I buried my mother it was also the best day of my life. I went back to my life knowing I could never be with Yurugobi." She gently shook her head, the brightness of her face dulled in the fire light. "I tried to reason with my father but he wouldn't hear of it. A few days later Yurugobi called for me, but he would never call for me again. I couldn't be subjected to another of his depraved acts. I had grown strong, strong enough to strangle the life out of him. At first he thought it was exciting, he encouraged it. He had done this to me before, he maintained it was fun and added to the excitement. However, he quickly realised that it was no game. He kicked, he punched but I held firm. I watched him die and I savoured every single second of it," She took a breath, "Even now after all these years the memory gives me pleasure, not for a moment do I regret taking that sick man's life, I would do it again in a heartbeat. Understandably his mother, Adeveima was distraught and wanted me killed as punishment. I sincerely believe that he would have done it had he not remembered that Yurugobi had raped me two or three years before. I was still awaiting my fate when a group of passing slavers offered to take me off his hands, for a small fee no doubt." Her face brightened, "The rest, as they say, is history, after several trades and lots of travelling I ended up as the prized possession of our former Lord Koranda." Matai looked into Tahira's eyes, "And now you know, oh and you can close your mouth now, it's not very ladylike!" She laughed.

    Tahira couldn't find any words to say but simply reached over to hug her friend and mentor.

TAHIRA THE ELEMENTAL

As was the custom at this point Matai offered to take first watch. Tahira teased her friend, "Will you actually manage to stay awake this time?" Matai swore her response as a smiling Tahira made herself comfortable before quickly falling asleep.

They woke refreshed and after breakfast began their exercises. Tahira made no mistakes this time and even suggested a run afterwards. Matai agreed but soon began to regret her decision. Was it that she was feeling her age? She still felt as strong as ever but this child seemed to be growing stronger by the day and was back at the camp fifty paces ahead of Matai.

In the afternoon Matai asked Tahira to attack her, and so self-defence school began. As expected Tahira got a kick up the back side but over the course of the hour or so the tables were turned. Tahira began to understand the various defensive approaches Matai was taking. She started to anticipate and counter Matai's tactics. Matai was strong but not strong enough against Tahira.

After a little break Tahira asked to learn about the throwing knives.

"Tomorrow," an exhausted Matai said as she made meal preparations, "But for now I want to know your story, how did you end up at Koranda's palace?"

As the day gave up the last of its light Tahira, with her hands cupped around a wooden bowl of broth, said, "There is not much I can tell you, my earliest memory is playing a game of stone walking. We lived as free men in a large stone building in the far north of Celta. I remember there were corridors connecting rooms and we would play a game of getting from one end of the hall to the other but you could only step on the same coloured stone." Realising that the story about a childhood game might not be what Matai wanted to hear she changed tack, "I never knew my mother and I have no brothers or sisters. My only family was my father. I don't know the details but one day my father came back to our sleeping quarters to say that raiders from the south of the country had arrived. He said that they were slavers and that we had to pack quickly as we were going on a journey. My father had worked for the local chieftain since my birth but the brigands had threatened to kill the chief and all his family and we were bargaining chips to ensure their survival. I remember these big strong men with swords placing us in the back of a wagon. My father believed that we were to be sold abroad but one of the raiders knew Koranda and thought that my father would be useful to him because he could speak many languages. As you know Lord Koranda was a powerful and wealthy man with lots of overseas connections, it suited him to own my father when trading with other tribes." She paused, "If my father knew what Koranda was going to do to me, I don't know what he would have done."

Matai noticed a tear fall from Tahira's cheek. It was now her turn to hug her friend.

The next day Matai laid out her throwing knives and invited Tahira to hit the trunk of a tree about ten paces away. She missed with each attempt. Having gathered them all up again, Matai demonstrated the technique.

"It's all in the wrist, the knives are weighted so by flicking the knife as you let go the blade will turn in the air to stick in its target. Now the key is to know how much to flick the knife, at ten paces you need to snap your wrist quite hard, like so."

TAHIRA THE ELEMENTAL

Casually Matai threw the knife. It hit the middle of the trunk about the height of a man's head. She took five paces further back, "At this distance you need less jerk." She released another knife. It landed a finger width away from the first knife. She took another five paces further and without saying a word, threw the third knife. Landing with barely any noise it split the gap between the two previous knives. "You need to create muscle memories, you need to get to the point where your only concern is to know how far your target is away and then let your subconscious take over, don't over think it. I have thrown these knives hundreds and thousands of times. I no longer have to think about the position of my wrist or how much flick I need to use. That's what you are aiming for, it will take a long time to get as good as me but you need to start somewhere."

Tahira practiced and practiced but struggled to make any improvement. This gave Matai plenty of time to tease her young companion. Tahira smiled through her gritted teeth but kept going. Matai rested and took the opportunity to nap. She drifted off to the sound of Tahira cursing under her breath.

When she awoke Tahira was bringing more firewood to the camp. The knives were nowhere to be seen. Next to the fire Tahira had placed a long thin stick which had three sharpened pieces of bone attached to one end with leather cordage. This had clearly been used to catch the two fish that were now sizzling on the fire. Matai didn't speak but the smell drove her to distraction. She devoured hers the second Tahira handed it over.

"You are a clever girl." Matai was handling the three pronged stick, "I seem to recall that my tribe had something similar but without the prongs. It was a thin sharpened stick, a bit like a short spear, but we had another piece of wood with a socket on one end, it was about two cubits in length. When you used it," she indicated a throwing motion, "it increased the power you could exert on the spear and so you could throw it much further, but it was very inaccurate so wasn't used much."

Tahira reached across and took the stick and then selected a piece of firewood with a small natural burr on it, "Like this you mean?"

They both watched as it sailed through the air over fifty paces to thud into the trunk of a tree. When Matai looked closer she could see her throwing knives embedded into the same tree in a circle formation with the diameter of a human head. The thrown spear was six inches below the circle.

"You are correct, it's not that accurate." Tahira smiled, "I think I prefer the bow and arrow." She casually reached behind her to where she had placed a small bow and the whittled arrows that she had made. She deftly sent one hurtling towards its target. It pierced the circle of knives.

"You can close your mouth now Matai, it's not very ladylike!" Tahira laughed.

"What, how?"

"Well you were so preoccupied with sleeping, all afternoon by the way, that I had to keep myself busy."

"Yes but, how long have you been an expert archer then?"

"Oh about an hour, I had to learn how to make one first, and I could only do that after I had perfected the knife throwing which took me a bit longer. I've known about the fish spear for months but had only just remembered about it now. It's so annoying, we could have been eating fish for days!" Tahira tutted, she lifted her eyes to the sky for added effect.

TAHIRA THE ELEMENTAL

Matai raised her hand, which was enough to stop Tahira speaking. "You are a young lady of many talents, we will leave tomorrow, I will take first watch."

Tahira wanted to explain, or at least try to explain. She kissed her necklace and settled down to sleep aware that Matai wouldn't believe her even if she told the truth.

"I am so proud of you Tahira, you are a much loved child."

The warm voice reverberated inside Tahira's sleeping brain. Tahira recalled the events earlier that day. She had grown so frustrated with the knife throwing exercise that she had become anxious. Subconsciously she had held her necklace in her hand and taken several deep breaths to calm herself down. She recalled how at this point her inner voice spoke to her. The same warm voice that had just spoken to her now in her dreams. She had felt it take over her body. Her inner voice and her own were as one. Her body relaxed. She had felt the knives leave her hand with a controlled flick of her wrists. She remembered how she had moved positions, closer and further away from her target. In what seemed like no time at all she almost mechanically was able to hit her intended targets without fail. She fancied she could do it in the dark such was her increased confidence.

She had then been shown a vision of a bow and arrow. The construction came to her instinctively. She was an expert fletcher and an even better shot. Again, it felt completely natural to her. The skills that craftsmen had taken several years to acquire had been gifted to her and she had quickly learned to use them well.

Rough Seas

After a couple of days travelling they approached the Port of Dour with a mix of excitement and trepidation. There were fewer than a hundred buildings of various styles and with varying degrees of effective construction.

They were generally ignored as they made their way along the high street towards the wharf as they were fortunate to arrive on market day.

Having noticed a horse trader Matai and Tahira dismounted. Matai handed some coins over to Tahira to buy some supplies of bread and cheese whilst she began the negotiations. She did not get the price she had hoped as the dealer had guessed that they were in town to seek passage to foreign lands. He did however give her the name of the captain of the trading ship that was currently in dock.

"Captain Felix, I presume?" Matai approached the big burly man with the long grey beard. He turned to face her and nodded before turning back to shout commands at a small gang of men in a language she did not understand. They carried on loading what appeared to be sacks of grain.

He spoke gruffly but as a clearly experienced trader he was able to communicate with her. "What do you want, sir? I don't need any more crew."

"We are looking for passage to Franecia, we will pay"

The captain turned back to his men. Picking one out Felix asked him a question. The response was immediate and caused a quick conversation between the two men.

Turning back to Matai he reverted back to a language Matai could understand. "One silver coin. Each!" Matai nodded and reached into her pouch and handed two pieces of silver over. Felix's big hairy hand snatched the coins from out of her outstretched hand. He bit them, "and another silver coin when we arrive!" His mainly toothless smile had a hint of menace. Matai should have been a bit more hesitant and should certainly not have shown her small coin pouch. Felix looked up to the sky before returning his gaze to the two 'men' standing in front of him. "The wind is picking up and we are approaching high tide so we will be leaving shortly, you will sleep on the foredeck, sir!" He bowed and pointed towards the front of his ship.

The sea state was calm as they left the port. They could hear bellowing commands from below decks and they could see the oars slapping into the water, each stroke propelling the ship forward. They cleared the sheltered natural harbour and entered the open seas. As they did so the crew unfurled the sails. The hoisted sails quickly filled with the strengthening wind producing a noticeable surge in forward momentum.

They settled into the rhythm of the ship's motion as it cut through the ocean waves. There was little to do so they alternated between silent daydreams and inconsequential conversations. There was no clear plan as it depended heavily on what they found when they set foot on solid ground. They would need horses that much they knew. Matai had wondered whether they might have brought their own horses with them but it was too late now.

There was little cloud around so as night began to cloak the sea, the light from the full moon shone bright enough to allow safe passage of the ship. Matai and Tahira tried to sleep but with little success. Not long before the anticipated sunrise a deck hand approached. "Captain Felix would like a word with you, if you please? He's down below, I will show you" He led Matai away leaving Tahira to guard their belongings.

Tahira heard the click of the latch on the door below where they sat.

"Knives. Now!"

She didn't hesitate, her hands where on the pack of throwing knives within an instant. As she got to her feet she felt a fist connect with her jaw, she stumbled as an unseen hand grabbed her throat. A swift upward strike with the throwing knife held in her right hand, accompanied with a quick twisting action caused her assailant to fall to his knees. He vomited blood as his eyes closed forever.

Another hand snatched at her hair pulling her backwards and towards him. His other hand had grabbed Tahira's right hand. He immediately wished he had a third hand as the knife in Tahira's left hand found its mark. Whether she got lucky or not he would never know. He was aware that he had been stabbed in his left groin. The blood now pouring from the open wound suggested that his femoral artery had been cut. He instinctively loosened his grip and staggered a pace back. It was enough for Tahira to be able to swivel around and with the knife in her now free hand she thrust it into his lower back, severing his spinal cord. The pain was intense but temporary. As he lowered his head Tahira slammed the knife in her left hand into his temple. He was dead before he hit the floor.

She heard the shouts of two more men running along the deck. The helmsman and his assistant had daggers raised above their heads. She waited and felt for the movement of the ship as it bounced along on the waves. She closed her eyes and sent her agent of death to meet its target. The helmsman fell, his wide eyes desperately trying to understand what had happened. He could see the hilt of a knife attached to his forehead. He couldn't see the blade but, he could have guessed where it was if he had had the time for another thought.

The helmsman's assistant looked at the corpse next to him before turning his attention back to the young man standing on the foredeck not ten paces ahead of him. He lost a bit of confidence and decided that he might be best to go downstairs to seek further assistance. He quickly turned to head towards the door but he was dead before he took a single step.

Tahira removed the knife from her would be attacker's left ear. She admonished herself as she had been aiming for the mastoid bone an inch further to the right. She turned her attention to the dead helmsman and retrieved Matai's other knife.

Tahira opened the cabin door.

"Well you took your time." Matai's voice was mocking.

Tahira could make out the bodies of the Captain and his first mate. The neck of the first mate was positioned in an extremely unnatural and therefore fatal way. The captain on the other hand appeared to be wearing a couple of fetching but rather heavily blooded glass adornments. They were in the shape of broken wine bottles which had been professionally inserted into the two opposing sides of the captain's jugular vein.

Tahira inspected Felix's body, "Just the two then?"

TAHIRA THE ELEMENTAL

"Well I didn't want to waste another bottle." Matai held aloft a bottle of wine. She took a long swig.

Tahira smiled, "You might need to keep a clear head."

Matai followed Tahira out onto the main deck standing next to the helmsman's dead body. Tahira pointed to the large wooden grill inserted into the deck itself. A dozen pairs of eyes were staring back up at them as the first light of the dawn caressed the rocking ship.

As Matai opened the grill she heard a lone voice begging for mercy. Her eyes adjusted to the improving light. The men were dirty and sweaty. It smelt awful and then she saw the chains.

"We need water," shouted one of the men, "We haven't had anything to drink in twelve hours."

Tahira had already passed Matai and busied herself giving out cups full of water. She also found a wooden box full of ship's biscuits which the men gratefully accepted.

"So what are you going to do with us?" the rather eloquent voice belonged to a young man with brown eyes. The voice also indicated someone high born.

"Shut your mouth Amir, we don't need any trouble." The voice belonged to the first man that spoke.

Matai calmly walked over to the impertinent Amir.

"Well, my dear, Amir, that depends really, you've seen a little sample of what my friend and I can do, remember the ones above deck had weapons, you do not."

Amir nodded. He flinched as Matai theatrically swept her hand perilously close to his face as she reached into her pocket and pulled out the captain's key. As she freed Amir she handed him the key whilst she and Tahira went back up on deck.

"Do any of you know how to sail this thing?" Of the dozen men now standing in front of them only two raised their hands. "Well that's a start at least. Can we try and get to dry land today please? Also you might want to freshen yourselves up. No offence, but when we arrive at our destination, wherever that may be, you might want to look like sailors and not slaves. There are plenty of good wearable clothes worn by, the former crew, alternatively, there is a chest in the captain's cabin full of other suitable attire."

From inside the captain's quarters they watched as the men selected their attire having thrown the bodies over board. Matai played particular attention to the men as they stripped naked and washed themselves with buckets of cold water.

"We should give them some privacy." Tahira chided her companion as she averted her eyes.

"Yes you are absolutely right. They should have a little privacy." Matai stepped through the door and onto the main deck. She made some mental notes as she passed them by and made her way to the new acting helmsman.

"Are we heading due south?" Matai asked her helmsman. He was nervous. These two strangers had readily defeated a team of experienced and hardened seafarers. Was he next on their list? He had the good grace to avert his eyes before nodding his assent.

She made her way back to the captain's quarters paying particular attention to a man with dark, short cropped hair and striking blue eyes. He appeared to be a broken man slightly younger than her, but, there was something about him. She gently reached out and took his hands and examined them carefully, turning them over. He didn't resist.

TAHIRA THE ELEMENTAL

"Would you be kind enough to tell me your name sir?"

"Lucretus, my lord!" He was quietly spoken.

"Ah Lucretus, please, there is no 'my lord' on this ship anymore, we are all equal." Matai was a little embarrassed. She was definitely no 'lord' even though she had to admit she had been quietly enjoying her role as self-appointed leader. "My name is Matai and my travelling companion is Tahira." She pointed to Tahira who had just come out of the captain's room holding a couple of items. Tahira had also changed clothes. She blushed as she felt the weight of all the men's eye's upon her.

"Please come with me Lucretus." Matai headed off back to the room at the front of the ship. Lucretus duly followed.

"That's a rather fetching outfit for a young man, Tahira?" Matai was somewhat confused. Tahira was standing next to an open chest full of clothes clearly designed for figures other than male. Matai looked inside, they were beautiful. Without batting an eyelid she stripped off and tried on a couple of things before settling on her new look. Tahira pointed towards Lucretus as she did the final button on her top which now covered her previously exposed breast.

"Would you like to try on some clothes Lucretus, or whatever your actual name is?"

Lucretus smiled, "I am not sure what you mean, my lord."

Matai invited Tahira to look at the hands of Lucretus. Again she did not resist as Tahira agreed, "Woman's hands!"

"She," Matai emphasised the point, "also did not get changed or washed in front of the other men. All that time she kept her eyes firmly on the sea."

Pirate Princess

There was a violent lurch of the ship as it came to a sudden halt causing all three to stumble as they ran out of the room and onto the main deck. There was a lot of shouting and cries of anguish as they had run aground on a sand bar.

"You get the sail down now, you four get down below and ready the oars, take the last four positions, Amir, can you help anyone the injured please?" Lucretus' voice was loud and commanding. She looked over the port side. The sandbar was two or three feet below the current sea level. They were still being buffeted. She turned once again and ran down the deck to help lower the sail.

Once done she turned to the helmsman, "Can you drop the kedge anchor now." In line with the other men he did as he was ordered without question.

She quickly went over to Amir. His update revealed that there was some bruising and cuts to a couple of the men but nothing serious.

Other than the standard rocking motion the ship was steady as she ordered the oarsmen. "Get ready below, I need you to reverse oar on my command." She went back to gaze over the port side as Tahira grabbed Matai by the elbow and led her down below to sit next to the oarsmen. "Now!" screamed Lucretus.

They pushed and pulled with all their might. Nothing, they remained stuck in the sand. They tried again but still nothing happened. They were now quickly joined by both Amir and Lucretus. Again they tried. Did it yield ever so slightly? It gave them hope and with a final strength sapping flourish they released themselves from the sand demon to the sound of cheers of joy and relief.

Lucretus quickly congratulated everyone for a job well done. She spent a little bit of time with the helmsman offering encouragement and tips rather than the admonishment he was expecting. There were more instructions given to the men in raising the sail. Matai and Tahira watched from the cabin.

"I knew they were women." Amir offered some water to Lucretus once everyone had settled into their roles, "The way they carried themselves, also they smelt different, you know, clean."

Lucretus smiled, "Amir the Healer is an expert in the fairer sex is he?"

Amir was defensive not realising that he was being teased, "Well, as a Court Physician."

"Ex court physician, also, weren't you more of a neophyte my young friend?" Lucretus laughed, Amir's discomfort was plain to see.

Realising he was being teased Amir poked his tongue out at his tormentor, "Well I might not have been fully qualified but as the son of a respected Court Physician," he carefully emphasised the point, "my father, may he rest in peace, taught me from an early age, anyway it was no secret that I knew more than my so called master."

Lucretus took a more conciliatory tone when interrupting him, "Look no one doubts your skills. You just need to learn to control that tongue of yours."

TAHIRA THE ELEMENTAL

He shrugged his shoulders, "Look all I'm saying is that although I'm only eighteen I was not surprised by the fact that our 'new friends' turned out to be women."

"Let's hope for your sake, that there are no more surprises then eh?" Lucretus hugged Amir before heading off towards the Captains room fully aware that Matai and Tahira had been carefully watching every move from the small glass windows on either side of the door.

"Land ahoy!" The man positioned at the front of the ship shouted his alert. Lucretus changed direction and quickly joined him. Scanning the horizon they agreed to head towards what looked like the opening to a river inlet. The man went back to the helmsman with the instructions.

Lucretus opened the cabin door to be greeted by two women grinning from ear to ear. Tahira offered Lucretus a hot drink.

"Pine tea?" The rich woody spiciness was unmistakeable.

"Elita, my birth name is so long that I barely remember it but I grew up being known as Elita. I am the youngest daughter," Elita smiled as Matai and Tahira nodded their formal greeting. The pause was only brief, "As I was saying, I am the youngest daughter of the King of Juteria."

"Juteria? As in the people of the Ice and Snow? I have heard tales about the Jutes being the Masters of the Sea and that your children first learn to walk on a boat but I thought it was just all legends and myths, tales told to frighten your enemies." Tahira was speaking excitedly, "My dad used to tell me about some of the things you would do to anyone who crossed you. When I misbehaved he would say that he was going to give me away to the blood thirsty Jute devils." Matai continued to look bemused. "So is it true that you drink the blood of your battle victims?"

Elita's striking blue eyes widened as she laughed loudly before whispering, "Only the fat ones, their blood is a bit thicker!" She laughed loudly again. Tahira realised that maybe her father's tales weren't quite as truthful as she had been led to believe.

"Well Captain Elita, what are your orders?" Matai stood up and offered a salute.

"Aren't you the captain of this ship now? We are merely slaves and under pirate law we are now at your mercy." Elita, although of a slim build, cut an imposing and confident figure with her short cut blonde hair. She had chosen this more masculine hairstyle so as to avoid standing out in the crowd. But, this was a new experience. Two women had dispatched a hardened crew of men with relative ease. Maybe the world was beginning to change. She, however, remained cautious of every promise and utterance from people she barely knew.

Matai threw a leather purse onto the table, several silver and gold coins spread themselves randomly across the oak planks. "This is the money that the, oh so lovely Captain Felix has left to you and the rest of the crew in his final will and testimony. I would suggest that you give each man enough for them to get home if they want plus a little extra but, you may want to keep some back for yourself to employ new crew." She looked over to Tahira who quickly nodded back. "Under your, so called pirate law, the former captain bequeathed his ship and cargo to Tahira and myself. This is not something we want as we intend to continue with our travels to the desert lands of the far south. You have shown that you are more than capable of handling this ship and its crew, also I suspect that the Jutes are actually Masters of the Sea and, that this is second nature to you." Matai leaned back in her chair, satisfied with her work.

Drinking the last of her pine tea Elita rose and walked over to the trunk in the corner of the cabin. She quickly rifled through it and selected a few items. Still with her back towards the others she quickly disrobed and put on clothing similar in style to that Tahira has chosen for herself earlier.

Tall goat skin boots tied just below the knee. Hers were brown, Tahira's were black. Her hemp based half trouser replaced with a pair made from fine ochre dyed wool. She had never worn a silk shirt before and it felt glorious next to her skin although she did acknowledge that the addition of a thin woollen undergarment was both warming and less 'exposing'. The hip length cow hide jacket along with a simple woollen hat completed the look. "Damn that feels better."

Turning her attention to the nearby bookcase Elita placed a rudimentary eyeglass into her pocket before walking back to the table with a map which she spread out for Matai and Tahira to see. "I accept your offer on one condition. I take you to the desert lands." She ran her forefinger along the image coastline, "It won't be easy but it will save you at least two seasons worth of travel and it will be safer of course," She looked across the table, "not for you, but for anyone stupid enough to cross you." Her smile quickly turned into a grin as both Matai and Tahira agreed it made sense. "Oh and we will rename this ship, Aija, in my birth language it means The Happy Falcon."

• • • •

There was a knock on the door and Amir entered. "We are nearing the entrance, to the," The words fell slowly from his mouth as he looked at Elita, "Lucretus?" He gulped.

Tahira seized the initiative and grabbing Amir's arm took him outside for a cosy little chat, "Have you lost your voice Amir?" she teased. She led him onto the bow of the ship to the sound of laughter from Matai and Elita.

They waited for the high tide before lifting their anchor and rowing themselves into the tiny little port on the northern Franecian coastline. It was protected by a small timber built fort. If anyone was on duty they were keeping themselves well hidden. The jetty was small but of a good solid construction.

Debarked tree trunks had been driven into the mud and stabilised with large boulders and rocks. These acted as the piles for a wharf creating a landing area for loading and unloading cargo.

If they were expecting a large crowd of onlookers they would be disappointed. Eventually an officious man with an armed guard arrived. He made a show of looking around the ship before returning his gaze to Elita. He spoke words which Elita did not understand. She looked at Matai for help.

"Sorry but we don't speak your language." Matai tried to give it her best quizzical look.

The man uttered a curse before repeating his previous enquiry whilst lifting two fingers in the air.

This time he received a reply. Tahira approached him and handed him two small silver coins. She spoke fluent Franecian, "I am sorry sir. Our captain is feeling sick at the moment and is confined to his quarters. He has asked me to pay the tax that is due and begs your permission to unload our cargo of grain."

TAHIRA THE ELEMENTAL

The harbour master took the money and scuttled away. Dealing with women was not something he was used too. The men began to unload their cargo as three merchants approached the ship. Once more they spoke in a language that only Tahira seemed to understand. Tahira stood by as the men checked the cargo. This was followed by an intense debate until there was just one man left. He handed over several coins before Tahira left him alone.

As she boarded the ship she suggested that they make haste while the tide is still high and leave before anyone started asking questions about the sick captain. By the time they had turned the boat around the successful bidder had loaded all the grain into carts and gone. Once more nobody paid them any attention as they rowed out of whatever sleepy little port they had just visited.

"I didn't know you could speak their language." Matai admonished, "You could have helped me the other day with Captain Felix."

"Well first of all you didn't ask, secondly why should you have all the fun and thirdly, I told you that my father spoke several languages well I'm not just a pretty face you know!" Tahira turned to face Elita, "Our friendly merchant was warning me about pirates as there are reports that some trading ships have had their cargo stolen and crew killed or enslaved, I can't imagine anything like that happening around here, can you?"

"That's fine we'll hug the coast and hope we get lucky. We will need to stop to get supplies from time to time. Also a few of the men want to go home now that they have had a taste of freedom, I've promised to drop them off next time we make land."

The next few days passed of quietly. There was a rhythm and routine to daily life on board. Elita busied herself teaching those that were going to stay on board how to handle the ship and what to do in emergencies. Tahira would join in the lessons and quickly became the best and most able student. Matai showed little interest in this side of things preferring to keep her knives sharp in between frequent bouts of exercise.

Tahira's instruction was not confined to her waking hours. At night her inner voice would come to her. Her dreams were filled with fire and flame. Her lessons included, how to manipulate the raw energy needed to make fire, how to make the particles move faster and faster, how to ignite that energy and finally how to control the resultant flame. She would practice when no one was looking but with only a limited amount of success.

On the fourth day they found a small natural harbour and were able to safely beach their ship. It would be several hours before the next high tide which would lift them clear of the sandbank. The four men who wanted to go home left on foot with the added bonus of an extra couple of coins from the sale of the grains.

They also took the opportunity to get some fresh water on board. Amir volunteered to go with Tahira in search of fresh game.

They arrived back in plenty of time, each carrying a stag across their shoulders.

"You should have seen her," Amir was telling the other sailors over supper that evening, "She moved without making a sound, it was like she was floating on air. The first stag was caught eating some food but as it dropped so it startled the other one which leapt into the air. The arrow thudded into it before it hit the ground killing it instantly."

The other men teased him, he was simply love struck and letting his imagination take over. They knew she was good with knives but very few men were capable of what Amir was describing let alone a woman.

The ship had separated into two groups. The women took over the captain's cabin whilst the men had the below desk area all to themselves when they weren't working. If any of the men resented that particular disparity of accommodation they never raised it. They were after all free men and could come and go as they pleased. They created little sleeping compartments for themselves below deck with one of the men using strips of hemp rope to fashion a net that if hung safely at each end provided an ideal hammock for sleeping.

The girls needed no such thing as there were four small single beds in the old captains quarters lined with a straw filled mattress in each. There hadn't been any discussion but they naturally took turns at keeping watch, as did the men.

With warm sunny days and little wind their progress down the coast was relatively slow. Matai began to grow restless. All she had known for the last fifteen years or so was hard work as well as certain night time activities. Although she revelled in her new found freedom and the companionship of Tahira and the others she was developing an itch and she knew that she would soon have to scratch it.

On the morning of the seventh day aboard their ship Matai awoke to the smell of pine needle tea and fresh warm bread.

She wasn't aware that Tahira had finally managed to light the required fire via mental projection. Tahira was beginning to understand the 'how to' side of her night time instructions. Whilst she was pleased she was also incredibly aware of how much energy it took out of her.

Elita had been on watch since first light and the smell of pine tea had drawn her to the cabin for her restorative breakfast. She had begun to sense the restlessness in Matai and wanted to get her to engage more in the running of the ship, so while they had their breakfast she spread the rudimentary map across the table.

"As you can see," Elita ran her finger across the map, "there is a huge bay ahead of us. I reckon it will take us three or four days to cross it if we hug the coastline as normal. However if we cut across we can be at the other side by the end of the day. What do you think Matai?"

Tahira noted that the question was not addressed to her and aware that Matai appeared distracted gave her an encouraging nudge in the shoulder.

With a quick apology Matai surveyed the map. Desperate to speed the journey up she quickly agreed to the change of tactics. "It will be a good exercise for the men to test out their newly acquired sailing skills in the deeper water and hopefully stronger winds."

The wind did indeed pick up as the morning progressed. The deeper water also produced more swell with bigger waves. The ships' company went through their drills and exercises. It was as if the ship had been longing to be out on the ocean. It cut through the waves with ease, like a falcon through the air. Free from worrying about potential inshore sandbanks the speed picked up. Matai had positioned herself at the bow of the ship. The cold sea air and the occasional sprinkling of salt water made her feel more alive than she had been for days. She felt invigorated as she shouted angrily into the wind, "Father, I'm coming home!"

The words were lost on the strengthening breeze as Tahira approached, "Come quickly, we may have a problem!"

Joining Elita on the starboard side of the ship facing out into the deeper sea the three women were aware of a boat in the distance. Using her eyeglass Elita could make out two sails, and estimated it was about two to three leagues away. She suggested that it was a bit bigger and therefore faster than theirs. Other than that it didn't appear out of place. Tahira however was nervous despite both Matai and Elita trying to assure her otherwise.

"They'll be heading for a port somewhere along this coast" Elita was confident. The crew resumed their duties with the exception of Amir. He had picked up Tahira's concern.

As Tahira held the ships rail Amir tried to offer some reassurance and intuitively placed his hand on top of hers. She didn't move, "I learnt some time ago to trust my inner voice and," she left the end of that sentence unfinished. She paused briefly unwilling to reveal anymore, "Anyway, thank you Amir." She moved her hand away, "I hope your confidence is not misplaced."

Amir hadn't heard her last words. He had touched her and she had not recoiled but there was something else, he felt a warm tingle through his body. It pleased and frightened him in equal measure.

It was early afternoon when they started hearing the drum beat. The ship on their starboard side was clearly visible and less than a league away. It was nearly twice the size of their little trading vessel. Elita ordered a slight change of direction. Still the drum sounded, an external heartbeat calling for action. The large vessel now changed direction, it mirrored theirs.

Once more Elita took out her eyeglass. She could see something metallic, shining in the sunlight, on the actual prow of the ship. She had heard tales from her youth. Did the drum beat get a little bit faster? Looking again she saw the row of oars scything through the sea in unison. They were gaining on them with every stroke. There must have been fifty oarsmen. The synchronisation of their movement to the sound of the drum was mesmerizing but Elita needed to act fast.

"Pirates!" She screamed at the top of her lungs, "They're going to ram us!"

All hands were quickly on deck, waiting for her commands. "Drop the sail." The drumbeat got faster. She handed her eyeglass to Tahira.

"But we are a sitting duck without our sail!" Amir voiced the concerns of the crew.

"I know, and that's what they will think too, now get below, all of you and man the port side oars only. Tahira stay with me." Matai wanted to object but thought better of it. "Now, do it!" Elita's commanding voice halted any internal objections the crew may have had. They ran below and manned the oars. She moved to the ships helm and turned her attention to Tahira, "When they get within three ship lengths they will withdraw their oars. When you see that you shout to the men below to row harder than they have ever done in their lives."

TAHIRA THE ELEMENTAL

Tahira nodded her understanding and turned back to face the onrushing ship. The metal ramming cap was now clearly visible. Still the drum boomed. Below decks they were all nervous, Matai did her best to calm the situation and try to get the men focused. She had no idea what the plan was. She had all too readily agreed to take this riskier short cut just so she could get home sooner. Her restlessness had endangered the crew and her friends. Although she didn't like the feeling of guilt she was experiencing she determined that she would rather live with it than die without it.

Tahira watched as the oars were savagely pulled back into the oncoming vessel, "Now!" Tahira screamed at the top of her lungs. Elita turned the helm, pointing the rudder towards the ramming ship. The crew pulled on the oars with all their might. They could hear the pirate's shouts and battle cries. They felt wood hit wood. But it was only a glancing blow. They had managed to turn their little boat almost ninty degrees. The larger vessel could not react in time. The contact was minimal but they were not out of danger yet. It wouldn't be long before the overshooting pirate vessel was turned around in order to try again.

"Burn." the word came unbidden.

"Burn, the sail, burn."

Tahira was not confused this time round but she had her doubts. When Lord Koranda threatened her she had no control over the flame. Something or someone else had taken her over and burned everything that they touched. A tiny spark to light a flame was the most she had conjured. She was panicking; this was more than she could do.

"Burn!"

The pirates had turned their ship around. The drum began to beat again as the oars were placed back into the water. It was slower this time round. This time they wouldn't ram the ship they planned to board it. The pirate crew displayed their weapons of choice.

"BURN!"

She had to try. She closed her eyes. Over the shouts of the pirates Tahira repeated the mantra, *take the energy, mould the energy, use the energy,* nothing happened!

Elita joined the crew below decks. Now splitting the rowing across both the port and starboard side she hoped to try and outrun them but without the sail they were simply playing for time.

"Focus."

The sounds drifted away, Tahira was alone with her thoughts. Once more her inner voice spoke, *"Good, now, take the energy, mould the energy and use the energy."*

Tahira created the mental image of a small ball of flame, hovering just above her outstretched hand. She pictured a ship with two sails. She pictured the small fireball leaving her hand and travelling to the first sail. With her left hand she recreated the vision hitting the second sail. And now a fireball hit the deck and another hit the stern setting the helm alight. Another slammed into the bow of the ship. She envisioned a rudderless ship, engulfed in flame as it drifted away to its watery grave.

"You have done well, my child." Darkness surrounded her as the voice faded. Tahira passed out.

Homecoming

"Oh good! You've finally decided to come back to the land of the living." Amir was busy mopping Tahira's forehead. Elita stopped pacing around the cabin.

She sat up in her bed as Matai handed her a pine tea, "Is everyone OK?" she asked.

Matai quickly responded, "Everyone is fine, thanks to you."

Amir injected, "Well everyone that is, apart from those bastard pirates."

Elita shot him a withering look. He did however have the grace to look embarrassed acknowledging his lack of diplomatic skills had let him down again.

"There must have been seventy, maybe eighty men on board." Tahira had picked up on Amir's reference.

Matai was quick with her reply. She needed to counter any guilt that Tahira might develop, if only as a deflection for the guilt she felt herself. "Look, you know that you acted out of self-defence. It's like having to deal with Captain Felix and his mob all over again. If those pirates had got on board this ship, do you think they would have spared our souls? Yes we could have taken several of them with us but there were too many, even for the great Matai and Tahira." The flourish at the end served to try and lighten the mood.

Tahira did smile, she knew that it had to be done but sending people to their grave was not something she enjoyed.

"Anyway, I don't know what made you think of it but, what a great idea to use the eyeglass to magnify the sunlight and set the sails on fire, genius." Matai secretly gave Tahira a wink.

Handing the drink back to Amir, Tahira closed her eyes, "Five more minutes would be good."

Amir wanted to stay to care for his charge but Matai and Elita were having none of it. Maybe he was slowly learning but he accepted their suggestion and busied himself elsewhere on the ship.

It was mid-afternoon by the time Tahira surfaced. "Still sharpening your knives Matai, I'm surprised there's any metal left on them."

"Mm, glad to see that you are still alive, I think!" Matai rushed over to give her companion a hug.

"So do you want to talk about it?" Matai had been biding her time. They had just finished their evening meal and Elita had left them to work with the helmsman to find them a sheltered spot to spend the night. Although travelling at night was possible under a full moon her crew were not yet ready for such a step. Sailing during the daylight hours and mooring in a sheltered spot at night was definitely the easiest and safest way to make progress.

Tahira hesitated, "No not really, there isn't much to say."

"Oh come one Tahira, this isn't about your prowess as an archer or knife thrower, this is something more, other people might buy my story about the eyeglass but if they knew what happened at Lord Koranda's place they would quickly put two and two together." Matai's tone was calm. She wanted to be supportive and not confrontational.

Tahira was shaking her head, "But I can't explain it, if I told you, you would think I am mad."

"Try me, oh wise one." Matai bowed flamboyantly making Tahira smile before sighing heavily.

TAHIRA THE ELEMENTAL

"I hear a voice inside my head," She paused briefly, "I know that sounds weird but when it speaks to me it feels as real to me as you are. It knows me but it is not me. For as long as I can remember I have had what I call my inner voice. When I was a child it was always there like an invisible friend but since I became a woman it changed, it now comes to me mainly at night but not every night. It teaches me things while I sleep and I feel safe and protected by it but, when that bastard Koranda attacked me I became almost blind with anger. There was grief for my father, utter frustration at my situation and a sheer loathing for another human being which I had never experienced before." There was desperation in her voice. She forced herself to take a long breath to calm herself down. "Just when I thought I was going to explode my inner voice came to me, it took me over, it was both exhilarating and terrifying, I felt total love as well as complete hate," Tahira paused thoughtfully, "It was a similar thing yesterday."

Matai responded, "My people believe that sometimes spirits get trapped inside our bodies. We have a shaman in our village. We should ask him, when we get home, to exorcise the demon that possesses you, but for now we shall celebrate your success in keeping us all alive, even if you are going a little bit mad." Using her forefinger she pointed to her temple and made a circular motion with it.

Tahira smiled along with her friend. She had been careful not to let Matai know the full truth. Yes her inner voice had killed Koranda. But there was no doubt that she had created the fireballs that had sent the pirates to their death. It was Tahira herself that had felt that power, she was no longer subservient to it, she, was now its controller, a true champion of elemental fire and, it felt good.

• • • •

As the land of Franecia turned and headed towards the equator the coast was less jagged and dramatic. There were more beaches but fewer ports. Elita's ship and novice crew hugged the ever changing coastline. They had no goods to trade and little desire to attract attention from the few ports that they passed by. They did see a couple of other trading vessels of similar size but no interaction was sought or given. With regular stops to refresh water and food supplies the next sixty days passed without incident.

Tahira had spent some time each day with Amir. She explained that it was to learn some of his medical practices whilst Amir hoped it meant something more. Tahira was impressed with his level of knowledge as a healer. Amir, however, was in awe. All the skills his father had taught him over his albeit short lifetime where readily picked up by this young woman. Not only did she understand, she was able to suggest techniques and practices to improve the treatment of patients, not that they had any. They would practice wound dressing and supports for broken bones on each other, or anyone else that happened to be nearby. It made him work even harder just to try and keep ahead. He of course did not know that Tahira was being helped every night by her inner voice.

The weather became noticeably warmer and the lushness of the fields and forests gradually waned. Life on board continued to be one based on routine with Elita spending time instructing the crew on ship maintenance. She ensured that the men had regular breaks. There were team building exercises with swimming races proving to be popular. Matai however became increasingly distant. When the first sand dunes could be seen from the ship she asked Elita to keep Aija at anchor.

"I will be leaving tomorrow." Matai's announcement at evening meal was expected by Tahira. This day was always going to come but even so Elita was not happy. The bond between them had grown strong. Matai had not only physically freed her from slavery but in so doing so had also removed the mental and emotional shackles that had previously held Elita back.

"Good! Myself and some of my men will escort you." Elita was determined.

"Absolutely no need, I will go by myself, I have to do this alone, my father will not like what he sees, and that includes you Tahira."

"No!" Tahira was standing. As she paced about the cabin her voice was respectful but firm, "We have come this far together, and, I won't let you face him alone, so, we will come along with you as your, oh I know," she was excited, "we will be your trading partners," she paused but only briefly and smiled, "you can close your mouth now, it's not very ladylike!"

Matai looked at Elita but the steely blue eyed stare she received gave no hint of potential compromise. She threw her hands in the air, "OK, OK, I can see that I am a fool to have two of the most stubborn people in the world to call friends but, can it just be us and leave the men behind, they will need to guard the ship after all?"

The debate carried on for most of the night. It was finally agreed that the trading party would consist of Matai, Elita,

Tahira and Amir, although his addition was more at the insistence of Tahira. The following morning they looked for a small river inlet in order to safely beach their ship.

The party of four headed due east along the river. It didn't take long for the cool onshore breeze to lose its potency. The heat was relentless but Matai cared not, she strode purposefully, within two days they should reach their destination. As the river became thinner so did the bankside vegetation. By late afternoon the river bed was dry. They saw little in the way of animal life so their evening meal consisted of dried meats and bread. As night fell so did the temperature. It was bitterly cold as they huddled around their fire. Under the clear night skies Tahira stared up at the sky and said hello to her mother and father 'stars'. She could have sworn that they shone just that little bit brighter as she drifted off to sleep. Matai took watch.

"Don't worry, they mean you no harm."

Tahira woke just as the first rays of sunshine kissed the sand. She quickly woke the others. Once more Matai was concerned to note that she had remained asleep despite Tahira having moved a few paces to wake her. She felt guilty that once again she had fallen asleep when on watch. But she was even more concerned, if not embarrassed, that she hadn't noticed the arrival of a group of aboriginal people who had managed to surround them.

Matai consternation was soon replaced with surprise. She was able to understand the group leader who spoke to her.

"It's OK," she explained, "They mean us no harm. We are clearly strangers and request that we present ourselves to their King, they will escort us."

TAHIRA THE ELEMENTAL

Seemingly from nowhere four camels appeared and they were invited to sit on their backs. Elita initially struggled, but quickly gained confidence. Amir was desperately trying to hide the fact that he was frightened. Tahira moved her camel alongside him to offer some reassurance before drifting back to ride alongside Matai.

Matai was staring off into the distance as Tahira spoke, "Well I definitely can't speak your language." Tahira smiled. Her words were enough to break Matai's train of thought.

"Yes, well I was a bit rusty," she paused briefly, "What is really weird though is, I learned to speak your Celtic language many years ago and now I am translating my native tongue into Celtish and then back again in order to communicate with our hosts. I mean I don't even think or dream in my own language?"

"So are we off to see your father then?" Tahira had expected Matai to be more agitated given the history between her and her father.

"Oh no, we are in the neighbouring tribes territory. We will be presented to their King tonight as night falls. If it had been my father's tribe they would either have taken us prisoner or killed us while we slept."

"Oh that's good to know." Tahira smiled playfully.

••••

The feasting and dancing had continued for over two hours. The people spread before them a large selection of fruits, cooked vegetables and exotic meats, many of which were unknown to the fascinated Tahira. Her heart was lightened by the sight of red dressed men, women and children jumping in unison in time to rhythmical drumbeats. Their arms were fixed to their sides as they leapt into the sky as if trying to reach the moon. As this display ended so female voices sang songs that were unintelligible to her but their soaring chorus brought other dancers to the fore providing interpretations of the meanings to the songs.

As darkness fell the only light was from the large camp fire. It flickered and crackled, it was a language that no one but Tahira understood. The small group of traders remained apprehensive. This was heightened when the dancing stopped abruptly at the sound of a loud whistle. There was a short pause. The silence was broken by a loud drum beat.

It repeated, slowly and regularly. The rhythmic pounding heralded the emergence of a few men from the largest mud built roundhouse in the village. Their faces remained in the shadows. They carried a highly decorated chair on which sat a human figure silhouetted against the night sky. As they moved towards Matai and her friends the villagers solemnly bowed their heads. Their deference indicated that they were about to meet their King. They sat his throne opposite Matai. He wore an animal skin and what appeared to be the mask of a big cat. He raised his hand and the drum beat stopped. The sound of silence was deafening.

One of the men standing next to the tribal leader spoke in a loud commanding voice. Matai, and the others, were surprised when he spoke not in her native language but in the language she had learned as a slave.

"Welcome strangers to our humble village" the crowd cheered, he raised his hand to demand silence, "As is customary we have provided you all with a welcome gift of this celebration." He theatrically moved his hand sweeping it across the village. The crowd cheered even louder. He quelled the noise. "It is also customary for our guests to provide our King with a gift as a sign of your good faith."

Matai quickly rose to her feet and walked confidently towards the seated King. She was stopped a few paces short by the other man on the King's left. He placed a large cushion on the ground. Matai bowed her head and placed her gift on the cushion and without turning her back on the King walked back to her group keeping her head bowed. She waved her hands to the others to indicate that they did not need to offer their own gifts. She had seen this ritual before and the symbolic nature of it.

As the cushion was offered to the King he reached out his hand and gently picked up the gift and examined it carefully. He stood up and bowed his head towards Matai before heading off towards his home. The gift had been well received, the villagers shouted as the celebrations continued once more.

"Was that another gold coin that you seem to have an ever abundant supply of?" Tahira was teasing Matai who simply smiled and undid the top buttons on her shirt, "Your necklace!" Tahira whispered but before she could say anything else Matai was approached by one of the King's aides.

"King Atalasian has requested a private meeting with you, if you would be so kind."

Matai rose to follow, she smiled at Tahira, "You can close your mouth now, it's not very lady like!"

Matai entered the dimly lit room to find Atalasian standing next to his ceremonial lion skin. He was lifting a paw with a missing claw. The one from the necklace he had been gifted fitted perfectly. He formally greeted Matai in their native tongue.

He next spoke in the trader's tongue. "You know I knew someone once," his voice was warm, almost soothing, "it was a long time ago and she was very special to me, but I digress, please indulge me, how did you come by this claw?"

Matai looked into the eyes of Atalasian, it was against protocol but she needed to see if the man she once knew was the same man that stood in front of her now.

She smiled, "Oh you know, it's a typical story of boy meets girl, they fall in love and then kill a lion. But their love can never be because they are from different tribes so they go their separate ways."

"Matai," he whispered, "Is that really you?"

• • • •

Tahira woke later than normal due to the late finish of the previous night's celebrations. Matai had not returned which was noted by Amir and Elita as they drank a pine tea.

"They are old, friends," Tahira was trying her best not to give the game away, "I'm sure that they had a lot of erm, catching up to do."

She went for a little walk around the village to get some fresh air. Walking past the campfire, which had gone out, she mentally created a spark and, making sure no one was watching, she pointed her finger at the fire which promptly relit itself. "Practice makes perfect." She said to herself.

The village was fairly large with over two hundred mud brick houses. The perimeter protected by a wide dead hedge made from spiky acacia branches. The dried inch long thorns that protruded along the full length of the pruned tree saplings made for an impenetrable fence. Any livestock predator would find it difficult and painful to get through. There were two gated entrances. She was standing near the one on the north side of the perimeter. From here she could see the oppositely placed southern entrance to the compound. Both were protected by guards armed with spears. Gazing back and out of the north gate she could see, mile after mile of dry sandy lands dotted with scrubby bush. The vegetation was relatively sparse but would provide enough food for their animals even through the dry season. In the far distance she could see a range of mountains, taller than any she had ever seen. The very tops where shrouded in mist and cloud. She walked across to the south gate to be greeted with a view of yet more arid land with scant vegetation.

When she returned to their guest accommodation she was pleasantly surprised to see Matai with Atalasian talking to Elita and Amir as if they were old friends. Tahira bowed her head in deference to meeting the Lion King.

He smiled and waved away her formality. "Thank you Tahira but, there is no need, the ceremony is for, visitors and traders alike." He now addressed the others collectively, "I would love to stay and get to know you all a little bit better and there will be time for this later, over tonight's evening meal maybe, however I must go and speak with my councillors, these are I'm afraid troubling times for my people." He squeezed Matai's hand before he left.

Tahira hugged Matai, no words were exchanged but she knew that Matai was happy and that was all she needed to know.

Matai suggested that Elita and Amir visit the market for provisions but to also talk to some of the merchants regarding items they could purchase and sell back in the lands further north. Atalasian has given his blessing to set up regular trade. His people made excellent clay pots along with lovely beaded jewellery.

All four walked together until they came to the northern gate where Matai and Tahira separated from them. They headed out of the village and made their way towards a small rock outcrop. Atalasian had informed Matai of a shaman who lived one league from the village in a natural cave. They arrived before noon.

The old man was blind but he didn't need that sense to 'see' who had arrived. He could hear a pair of footsteps. He could smell the pine scent on a woman's breath. Matai spoke a greeting in her native tongue. The medicine man was surprised when he was told that there were two women present as he had heard only one set of footsteps. He knew he was nearing his time but his senses had never failed him before.

He asked Tahira to follow him to a small hut outside of his cave. He blocked Matai from entering with Tahira. He asked her to wait somewhere close as it wouldn't take too long.

Tahira and the shaman sat cross legged opposite each other. They remained silent as he reached into a basket and sprinkled some of dust it contained onto a small fire. The fire was burning dried animal dung with a distinctive aroma. As the powder hit the fire the yellow flame dulled to brown before turning purple as a sweet smelling gas was released.

The old man began to shake and twitch as he drew deep breaths of the sweet almost sickly air. He remained silent as he transcended into dreamtime. Tahira remained calm. Her inner voice had already told her there was nothing to fear. She closed her eyes, as she did so the shaman stopped twitching.

Tahira had a vision. She was standing on a beach. On the landward side was a door. She could hear someone knocking on the door. With some difficulty she could peer around the door but could see no one. The knocking became louder. Then she heard a voice, she couldn't hear what was being said but it made her cross. Still the thumping got louder. The voice went from a whisper to a scream but she could not make out what was being said. Anger welled inside her. It was immediately replaced with despair and utter sadness. A tear rolled down her cheek. Then she smiled, she was happy. Her emotional rollercoaster culminating in a sense of complete and utter joy, she felt as if she was going to burst such was her pleasure. It abruptly ended with the return of the rapping on the door which was louder than before. The disembodied voice also returned, appearing to wrap around her like a vortex, a cacophony of sounds that wanted to reach out to her and consume her. Such was her desperation she grabbed the door handle but it wouldn't move. The anger inside her returned. She tried with all her strength but still nothing. She imagined a ball of fire in her hand, she envisioned it leaving her hand and striking into the door.

"*Ssh my child,*" her inner voice came to her, "*you are in dreamtime,*" it spoke quietly, "*you have much to learn,*" it was soothing, "*but for now this is over,*" it was calming, "*I need you to return to the land of the waking,*" it was loving, "*you are needed there.*"

The anger Tahira felt simply melted away. A calmness and confidence returned to her. Silence greeted her and as she inhaled softly through her nose she opened her eyes and looked into the dimly lit hut. The sweet smelling smoky air had gone. She looked at the old man opposite her.

Still seated his head was tilted backwards. With his mouth agape and his eyes closed he appeared lifeless. She was concerned and reached over to him. As she touched him so his body collapsed in on itself until all that remained was a pile of desiccated dust and bone. Tahira involuntarily screamed. It took her a few moments to compose herself.

She opened the door of the mud hut expecting to find Matai to come running to her rescue but she was nowhere to be seen. She didn't like it. Nervously she called out her name only to be greeted by the shrieks of vultures circling overhead. She called out again, then she saw some faint tracks leading to a nearby rock not twenty paces from the hut. It would be a good place to sit and keep an eye on the dreamtime hut. Tahira soon realised it was also a good place for someone or something to hunt with thick bush only a few steps further.

There was a speck of blood on the ground next to the rock. Worryingly she saw fresh tracks next to a human sized depression in the ground. She knew better than to call out again. She dropped onto her haunches. Carefully she followed the tracks into the bush.

As the bush cleared she found a large area of disturbed ground. There was evidence of camels, maybe four or five. There was more blood but it contained animal hair, a hunting party maybe. Then she saw a broken beaded wristband which she put in her pocket. She followed the tracks for several hundred paces until they diverged. The hunters had split up. One set of tracks showed a greater distance between the toe prints, these camels were running.

"Go to Atalasian!"

Tahira ignored her inner voice. She carried on following the tracks. The land became sandier. It became harder and harder for her to move on foot. Soon there was no vegetation in sight and the early afternoon sun poured its heat onto the arid and barren land.

"Go to Atalasian!" her inner voice was almost pleading.

Once more she ignored it. Struggling in the heat and with no water her running had become a walk. The sun continued to beat down upon her. Her dry mouth could no longer form words. Tiny grains of sands scratched away at her skin. She stumbled. Was her mind playing tricks on her? Was there something moving up ahead? She fell to her knees. A dark shadow swirled around her. She felt herself being lifted into the air before passing out.

• • • •

"Tahira, can you hear me." She woke to the familiar sound of Amir's voice. "Oh praise be given to the God of Life. You have come back to me." He quickly raised her up and gave her a herbal drink. Such was her thirst that she gulped it down.

"Matai," she whispered, "Matai, where is she?"

"We don't know, Tahira, we were hoping you might be able to tell us." Atalasian's voice was calm but edgy.

"We went to see the shaman," her voice was barely above a whisper, "when I came out she was gone, she had been attacked. Look!"

Atalasian was pacing about the room. Tahira reached into her pocket and retrieved the beadwork she had found and handed over to the king. He took it to the aide who had found Tahira wandering in the desert. Atalasian was desperately trying to control his anger. It wasn't his aide's fault, if the aide hadn't found Tahira they would be in a far worse situation. It was clearly a heated exchange. The victim of Atalasian's verbal assault bowed his head and left.

The herbal drink was having its desired effect. Tahira began to feel a bit brighter, more alive. Elita gave her hug.

Atalasian paused momentarily desperately trying to regain some composure as he re-joined the small group of traders near Tahira's bed. He sat with them and took a deep breath before addressing them in the language they could understand.

"My honoured guests and partners, these are, troubling times for my people."

"Where is Matai? You know don't you?" Tahira was in no mood for political talk, she wanted facts and she wanted them now.

"PATIENCE! Let him speak child!"

Tahira was startled into silence.

Atalasian adopted a more conciliatory tone but he was still The Lion King and they would listen.

"I suspect, someone, I have sent word to my spies for confirmation." He waved his hand in the direction of the now departed aide. "As I was saying, these are challenging times. Our neighbouring tribe has been on a war footing for a few years now. They have concentrated their efforts to the more fertile lands south and west of here but now, but now it would appear that their attention has brought our lands firmly into their sights." He quickly waved away the questions that Tahira was about to raise, "for a few months now we have had people and animals taken, they simply don't come home in the evening. I have resorted to paying informants from the other tribe and they have confirmed our worst fears, they are looking to seize land and property and enslave anyone they can capture. In light of this information I started sending out our own patrols, you were lucky that one of them found you, but now."

"But now, what?" Elita surprised herself by interrupting the King.

He simply raised his hand, "Well this is not your fight. You will pack up your things and two of my men will escort you back to your ship tonight."

"Not without Matai!" It was now Tahira's turn to interrupt King Atalasian.

"You!" The King rose from his seat and pointed a finger at the group, he raised his voice, "You have no choice, I rule this land and if that Dogon bastard has taken my beloved Matai I will have my vengeance, there will be war!" He stormed out of the roundhouse.

They looked at each before Tahira got herself out of bed. The exhaustion from dehydration was gone, but, she needed time to think and she needed to be alone. Amir wanted to object but looking into her eyes he quickly thought better of it.

The heat from the mid-morning sun almost took her breath away. She shielded her eyes and made her way to the gates at the southern end of the village. With a goatskin full of water she headed in the direction of the sun and the tribal lands of the Dogon.

After walking for a league or so she arrived at a small bluff. It was covered in small acacia like bushes giving her a little bit of shade and respite from the blazing sun. The escarpment was barely as high as two people but it looked out over a massive flat plain. It was so big that she couldn't see the end of it in any direction. The area seemed alive with several small camps in the distance. There were plumes of smoke suggestive of people going about their daily lives. These were interspersed with dust clouds from the animals that they were keeping.

"Why are you so disobedient child? You know that I want to help you."

Tahira was taken by surprise. The conversation was unwanted and unwarranted as far as she was concerned. "Go away." She hissed.

"Oh I can't do that my dear, nor would I want too, please can we talk?"

The troubled teenager didn't answer and sulkily sat on a small rock out of sight, but, with a clear view of the land before her.

"Well it's a start I suppose." There was a short pause, *"Look deep into your heart and focus on Matai, think of how she looks, how she talks, how she feels, close your eyes and concentrate."* Her inner voice was calm now, soothing almost hypnotic. *"Good, that's very good."*

Ba-Dum, Ba-Dum. Tahira didn't hear the incredibly faint sound but she did feel it. Ba-Dum, Ba-Dum. There it was again. She didn't need to ask. Matai was alive, but how?

"Everything and everyone is, connected, you, me, Matai, the land, the moon, the sun and the stars are all connected through

energy. Energy is the life force of the universe, a connective tissue reaching out like a spider's web."

Tahira understood. It confirmed half formed thoughts and theories that had whirled away in the far recesses of her mind. She had dismissed them as mere fantasies and illusions. Ever since she was young she had a sense of being different from other children. Their childish games had soon bored her. She preferred the company of her father and other adults. They had knowledge and she was a quick learner. And now this revelation and her experience with fire, it made sense to her, the final piece in the puzzle. Her mood lightened until she brought her thoughts back to rescuing Matai.

"But look, you don't know where she is."

"She'll be in one of those small camps, I know it. I could easily..."

"If?" Her inner voice interrupted, *"If they were small camps or farms then yes but, look again, think about how far away they are. Also, those clouds of dust you can see, they are not animals as you suppose they are in fact warriors preparing for war. You cannot defeat them all, not yet, you are not ready."*

"But I could send fire to them." Tahira took another look. She had to accept that she had been too quick to judge. She had expected to see animals so she saw animals. Instead, what she now saw were thousands of people scattered across the plain. There had to be eight to ten times as many people as Atalasian had at his disposal. A direct confrontation would lead to a massacre of the Lion Kings tribe.

"There are too many, it would take all of your life force before you got even a quarter of the way through them, remember how fire takes away your own energy, no, you need to take a different

approach, think of the shaman and what happened to him after he died."

Tahira cried out, "But I killed him and then turned him to dust. I didn't even know I was doing it. He didn't deserve to die by my hand. He was supposed to be helping me."

"No. You didn't kill him. In fact you were actually helping him. Look, he was dying, he knew it himself. When he entered dreamtime with you he knew he would not come out of it alive. The knocking on the door was his heartbeat. You felt his lifetime of emotions condensed into a minute of time. He rapped on the door again begging you to open it for him so he could move onto his next life. In the moment that you smashed the door down his life ended and he was able to enter the spirit world." Her inner voice paused briefly, *"And it was me who turned him into dust."*

"So how does this help?" Tahira was confused.

"It was to be your next lesson but Matai's kidnapping has brought that forward a little."

Tahira's mind was a whirl. She took a deep breath and closed her eyes once more. She needed to concentrate. She needed to calm herself down and focus. It was clear to her that if she was to help Matai she had better listen.

"You know that you have the ability to use and mould energy, look what you can do with fire, but that energy has only been changed, even you cannot create or destroy energy but you can change its form, when I took the shaman's flesh and converted it to dust I was using a very visual way to show you that principle, but there is a price to pay, when you boil the water to make your pine tea you are using something else to create the heat, when you create a fireball it is your energy that is being used and it takes time for you to regain the energy that you have lost"

Once more her inner voice was telling her things that intuitively she knew were right. Each time she had used her ability it had come at a cost to herself. She quickly reflected that it had taken her slightly less time to recover each time that she had used her skills but even so she had to accept that taking on so many people would kill her. She felt a sense of despair wash over her.

"I know you don't want to hear this but, sometimes you have to make sacrifices for the greater good, your priority has to be to warn Atalasian and save hundreds of lives."

Her inner voice remained silent as Tahira wept. After a few minutes and with a heavy heart Tahira rose and headed back towards the Atlantean village. She walked quickly and then broke into a run. She knew this would be what Matai would tell her to do but still it hurt.

Running on the loose sand was difficult and she stumbled more than once. "So can I make this loose sand firmer to make it easier for me to move on?"

"Yes, think about the grains of sand and then think about the air gap between them." Tahira stopped running to concentrate and focus her mind. This had worked before, *"Good, now think about moving the air away from each gap, remember it's not just the side to side connection but the sand grains above and below."*

Tahira opened her eyes and looked at her feet. The ground was solid. As she stamped her feet the last puff of air escaped. Whilst still looking at the ground she thought about pushing the air back into the gaps between the sand grains. Her feet sunk ever so slightly. She repeated the process several times before setting out on her run back to the village.

She was back before night fall. Elita and Amir had packed their bags in readiness for leaving the village that night as Atalasian had requested. She asked Elita to go and find the King before requesting Amir to give her one of his special herbal drinks. She was beginning to feel the after effects of her use of 'magic' but needed to be conscious for as long as possible.

Atalasian angrily dismissed her concerns. His neighbour could not have amassed that many warriors. She was to be sent away along with Elita and Amir back to their ship. They would leave at midnight. Tahira was struggling to argue and simply ran out of energy and drifted off to sleep.

All was relatively quiet for a couple of hours but the air was thick with dread. Peering out of their door Amir started to notice that the firelights in the huts were being extinguished. It was a moonless night but he could still see people milling around. Hushed whispers in unfamiliar tongues.

"She's coming round Amir." Elita's voice broke Amir's sense of melancholy. He rushed back to Tahira's side. He offered her another stimulating herbal drink. She was just getting to her feet when Atalasian entered along with one of his aides.

He was angry no more. He was relatively calm but organised with determination in his voice. "I am sorry to inform you." He shook his head and looked into Tahira's eyes. "My spies confirm that Dogon has captured his daughter Matai, she is to be sacrificed at dawn as an offering to the gods for a successful war against my people, they have over 5,000 men while we barely number 600, I cannot allow my people to be massacred or enslaved by that, barbarian." Atlassia spat the last of those words out. Fear and loathing had been replaced by anger and rage. "You will travel with us, for your safety, by traveling now we should get several leagues ahead of them, that will give us enough time to make it to our new city in the mountains, it is nearly ready and we should be able to defend it more easily."

"That is a good plan my Lord Atalasian, you are wise to protect your people." Tahira's voice cut through the air like a knife.

"Then come my friends before it is too late, your camels are still outside waiting for you. My aide will guide you." Atalasian pointed to the door.

Tahira simply shook her head, "You go, with my blessing but sadly, I cannot. Matai is my friend and I have to do something."

"No, please Tahira, no, you are not ready, you have so much to learn."

Tahira hissed her internal monologue into silence. She had not intended it to be an audible noise but it did have the effect of silencing the commotion her previous utterance had caused.

Elita and Amir knew not to further challenge Tahira on this. They offered to help in some way but Tahira dismissed this as folly. It was bad enough that she was prepared to risk her own life. Risking others in her name was not something she could accept. They continued to protest as the aide showed them to their camels and their journey to the city in the mountains.

Stepping outside the hut Atalasian and Tahira could see that the busy village was now deathly silent. The last of the people had gone. The shadows in the distance were dark and foreboding.

"And now you can leave my dear Atalasian." Tahira was now standing at the southern gate.

"Good, I was wondering when we were going to leave." He deftly waved his hand and two guards appeared along with a wooden cart led by four camels. "They are my personal bodyguards and I cannot leave the village without them, like you they are very stubborn people."

Tahira smiled, she didn't have a plan but, "My King, your duty is to your people, they need you now more than ever."

Atalasian raised his hand to silence her. He spoke firmly, "My most honoured guest, despite what you have chosen to believe, I, Atalasian, the King of the Atlanteans, am fully aware of my duties and responsibilities towards my people, I do not need a young lady from a foreign land to come here and lecture me on what is the right, or wrong thing to do. You have brought the love of my life back to me and I cannot," He took a breath, "Cannot bear to lose her again, do you hear me? Do you understand me Tahira? This is not a game to me, my people will survive without me - my councillors will ensure it." Once more he paused thoughtfully, "We have been planning and building our new home for quite some time, this just brings the move forward a bit." Tahira nodded her understanding. He reminded her of her own father when he spoke about her mother Siria. Atalasian continued, "The question you need to ask however is, will I survive without my Matai? The answer is simple, no I would not!" His voice was now pleading. "I lost her once. I cannot and will not lose her again." Tahira smiled. His voice brightened, "Good, now can we leave?"

TAHIRA THE ELEMENTAL

They headed off at a controlled speed. The camels barely made a sound as they paced their way towards the escarpment. They quickly found a way down onto the plains. Tahira had wrapped herself in fine cloth covering any exposed and distinctively coloured flesh. They were stopped at one point by a small patrol but lifting the coverings in the cart to expose some pots and skins they were quickly accepted as traders and allowed on their way. A goatskin full of bull's blood wine helped smooth over any concerns the patrol may have had.

"Have you got a plan?" The king asked Tahira as they arrived and camped on the perimeter of the main camp of Dogon.

She shook her head, "No not yet. Did your spies tell you which of the huts she is being held in?"

Atalasian reached into his pocket. He unfurled a small piece of cloth. Using the meagre light, from the small camp fire they had set up, he showed Tahira the prison hut. It was the middle of 3 huts positioned at the near edge of the village to them. There was still however the small matter of a man high and a man's length of thick, thorny acacia bush to cross to get to the hut.

"Is there anything I can do or say to make you change your course of action?"

Tahira failed to answer. *"So be it my child, the only help I can give you is this, remember the shaman and how I changed him into dust, the acacia bushes are also dead so you could speed up their decomposition."* Tahira leapt to her feet and moved towards the bush barrier. She could set it on fire but that would only attract attention but changing it into dust. She imagined the dead cells, she imagined them being crushed, she imagined the tiny remnants falling to the ground.

She quickly returned to their makeshift camp, "I have a plan," Tahira whispered to Atalasian, "but we have to be very quiet and, we don't have long, maybe one hour until sunrise."

Tahira quickly turned on her heels and headed back to the dead hedge. Atalasian and his men quietly manoeuvred the camels and cart. When they arrived at the bush they were surprised to see that there was small gap about the width of man. Knowing what they needed to do next the three men entered the camp with Tahira taking the reins of the camel cart. Whilst she couldn't see what was happening she could hear faint muffled sounds. The two bodyguards were clearly adept at their job. Within minutes a battered and bruised Matai appeared being carried on the shoulder of her lover. She was unconscious. They placed her under various animal skins with Atalasian lying beside her to keep her warm.

One of the bodyguards took over the reins. They moved slowly and steadily not wanting to attract attention. Tahira concentrated and let her mind think about spreading dead acacia branches in order to close a certain gap in a certain hedge.

The air was still. The only sound they could hear was the padding of the camel's feet on the hard pan of the baked arid plain. The wheel bearings had been smothered in animal fat to ease their operation. They kept scanning the area hoping against hope that they would remain undetected.

They had barely covered half the distance to the rocky bluff when the first light of dawn spread its fingers across the land. They could just make out a small military camp coming to life not a mile away. Their camels would be fully rested and without having been encumbered by pulling a heavy cart they would quickly catch them up.

"We need to increase speed." Tahira commanded the driver. She immediately apologised to Atalasian for the bumpy ride. The pace quickened. Within minutes they heard the sound of a drum beat, and then another, and another. It rippled across the plain as each camp heard and responded to the alarm. War was afoot and they needed to get to safety.

As they reached the bluff Tahira whispered into the drivers ear and deliberately out of Atalasian's range, "Whatever happens, do not stop, do not turn around, do you understand, no matter what, you must get your King to safety, that is your duty yes?" The man nodded, surprised not only by what was said but also that it was in his own language, "You will also take Matai to my friend Amir as he will know how to make her better, again do you understand? Promise me!" Once more the man nodded and with that Tahira leapt from the cart.

With expert timing she completed two forward rolls and was on her feet in seconds. She quickly moved towards the familiar view point where she had spent some time the previous day. She beat off the dust from her clothes as the last of the sounds from the cart faded away. She peered through the bush and onto the expanse of plain below. The boom of the drum beat echoed all around. She could see that Dogon's people had begun to gather together. They were moving slowly towards her position on their way to battle the people of Atlantea.

She watched the hordes of men moving slowly and methodically flanked on either side by large groups of men mounted on camels. First the left flank would move ahead then the right would catch up and move forward before the left flank took charge once more. And so it repeated like a beating heart fully tuned to the sound of the drums. Behind the warriors Tahira could make out the supporting cast. It was a vast ensemble of the tribe's women and children. They were busy fetching and carrying whatever their chosen warrior needed. As it was the dry season the plain sent a small puff of dust up into the air with every footstep. It looked like smoke to her eyes.

She considered her options. She had to concede, a frontal assault would never work, even with her special abilities. In that moment she became afraid, in that instant the hopelessness of her situation hit her hard. She wanted to run, or hide maybe. She thought about Matai.

"Diversion and delay." She said to no one. This was not about her. She needed to find a way to give Matai and the Atlantean people enough time to find safety.

She imagined cooking pots and the fires on which they sat. She imagined how the fire could grow and then she thought about the heat from those fires. She thought about tiny embers being spat out of those fires and maybe onto the dried rush roofs of the Dogon village huts.

She opened her eyes and looked beyond the mass of warriors and their entourage. Billowing smoke was visible even from where she sat. Some of the women and children were sent back moving like columns of worker ants, desperate to prevent the fire destroying their homes. Still the main force of warriors kept moving forward, one step after another. They were at best a couple of miles away. She could hear individual voices, singing and chanting a 'calls to arms'. Their spears moved up and down to the rhythm of the drums. She could now just make out small shields that they carried in their left hands. Probably made from a hard wood and painted in bright colours.

The dust clouds appeared to grow. Thousands of tiny particles thrust into the air with each stomp of a warrior's foot. Each one having a brief sense of freedom before gravity exerted its power to bring it gently to rest on the ground. Once more it filled the miniscule gap between the grains of sand and dried mud awaiting the next opportunity to dance in the warm air.

Tahira imagined what would happen if all the dust particles were lifted into the air at the same time and blown into the faces of the men, women and children below. It was as if time stopped. Only the camels with their protective nictitating membrane remained unaffected. The people became disorientated.

Tahira imagined what would happen if the gaps between the sand and mud particles became wider. She focused on the land directly below her viewpoint and closed her eyes. She saw grains of sand and particles of mud being driven apart. Dust particles were swept up into the air. She pictured water from deep below ground seeping upwards to fill the newly opened spaces. She slowly opened her eyes. The land below had swollen in size about half the height of a man and had stretched out about two hundred paces towards the warriors.

The dust clouds were quickly reclaimed by gravity. Tahira drew even more energy from her limited reserves as the commanders barked their orders urging their men to move forward once more. The first few ranks trod on the raised land and immediately sank. Their bodies swallowed by the quicksand. Hundreds of men perished with their shouts of anguish cut short. They moved to the left and tried again but the quicksand was waiting for them, several hundred more men were engulfed before the retreat order was given. The drum beat wavered but not the resolve of the warriors. Changing direction once more the remaining army moved to the right only to meet the same fate.

This procession continued for the rest of the morning. Probing to find a safe passage but each thrust having the same fatal result. Each attempt sapped their morale but still they came. Each lunge drawing yet more power from Tahira but, still she worked weaving her imagination, desperate to give her friends time to reach safety.

Smaller numbers of men were risked each time but they all suffered the same unenviable fate. By midday the remaining exhausted men had lost over half their battle force. They began to pull back.

Tahira watched through tired eyes. As they retreated so did her adrenaline. She knew it would only be a matter of time before they regrouped and came again. But she was confident that it would be several months if not years before they did.

Her body needed to rest. Looking around she found a small cave she hadn't seen before. So many men had lost their lives because of her and yet what could she do? Without her actions more people would have died and/or been enslaved. Shaking her head she crawled inside. She made herself as comfortable as possible before crying herself to sleep. Unbeknown to her the cave opening closed.

"*Sleep well my child. We are so very proud of you.*"

City Of Atlassia

Tahira remained cocooned for several days. She was safe and protected. Her dreams were lucid but full of love and wonder. She learnt more about controlling fire and changing the state of matter.

"Time for you to go now my child, your friends are back at the village."

Tahira woke up as the first golden rays of sunshine warmed her skin. The cave was nowhere to be seen. She felt different somehow but alive and bursting with energy. She walked briskly back to the village of the Atlanteans.

Her heart dropped as she came to the realisation that the village was deserted. She heard the bleat of a nanny goat from the direction of the north gate. She ran quickly to see the last of a herd of goats being loaded onto a cart. The donkey that was to lead the cart made a braying sound as she approached. The goat herder looked at her suspiciously before a hint of recognition had him raising his eyes to the skies and offer up a prayer to whatever God he believed in. "Tahira, this is a blessed day, please come with me, I will take you to see your friends." He offered her some water and bread as the man's wife and daughter came out of the hut next to the gate. "My name is Amastan and this is my wife Kahina." He pointed to his daughter, "And this is Lunja." She smiled and bowed at Tahira.

Tahira bowed her head in response, before speaking in Atlantean, "Lunja, you are well named for there has never been a prettier fairy princess." Turning to Kahina she said, "I see she gets her good looks from her mother." Kahina smiled.

Tahira gratefully accepted the water from Amastan, "So where is everyone else?"

"Why we have moved to our new city in the mountains." There was joy in Amastan's voice.

A memory stirred. Atalasian had mentioned something about moving to a new home to avoid war with their neighbouring tribe. Without reason to distrust the goat herder and his family she welcomed the offer of a lift.

She could see the mountains far off in the distance but it still took them until late afternoon to reach them. They were majestic in their beauty but they were imposing and formidable, a seemingly impenetrable barrier. But as they trundled ever nearer the goat herder saw what he was looking for. It was not obvious, just a small gap in the rock barely the width of their cart. From her vantage point it looked like a dead end. Amastan however urged the donkey forward. They turned sharply left before quickly turning right. The track ahead rose fairly steeply. She felt claustrophobic and hemmed in. The passage had been hewn from black basaltic rock. The walls on each side stood as tall as a tree. These man made walls appeared to flicker with a green luminescence as the rays from the lowering sun danced across the surface. Reaching out Tahira allowed her fingertips to glide across the smooth stone surface. Lunja reached across her and pointed to one of the many sparkling flecks of the mineral olivine and said, "So pretty, just like your eyes." Tahira smiled.

As they climbed the mountain pass it veered to the right. Tahira then heard a rumbling sound of thunder, but the sky was still clear. Looking behind she could see a huge gate had been rolled across the pathway. She felt as though she was being watched. Amastan smiled and told her there was nothing to worry about, they were nearly home. The pathway began to turn to the left and they stopped at an imposing metallic gate. She had seen something similar at a large stone castle back in Celta. The gates were opened and they crossed onto a long wooden bridge. She felt sick as she peered over the edge and into a deep ravine that spread out in both directions. Before them was another huge gate. She noted how the gap between the rocky cliffs and the gate house had been filled in with large boulders of rock, presumably from the basalt that had been quarried out to make the path that she had just ascended. Once more the goat herder smiled as the gate opened to reveal a magnificent stone built city spread out in all its glory before her.

The guards at the gate came out to welcome her. Whispers spread throughout the city. Children came to see her, to touch her. As she smiled they smiled, she gave them blessings in their own Atlantean language.

Elita heard the name Tahira drift on the soft, warm breeze. She ran to her with tears of joy running down her face. She held her tightly squeezing the breath out of Tahira, "Thank the Gods in the Sky, we thought we had lost you," she released Tahira and took a step back in admiration, "Wow, just look at you, Atalasian has sent search party after search party looking for you, anyway you look, amazing, come on!" She grabbed Tahira's hand and they ran off together towards the tribal leader's dwelling. "Oh and whatever poultice you are using on your skin I want some!"

Matai was awake and desperate to hug her friend. Amir had tended to her well. She had some scars but the cuts and bruises were all healed. There was still some internal damage but Amir assured everyone that she would be OK. Rest is what she needed and lots of it.

Tahira held Matai's hand and looked lovingly into her old friends eyes. They didn't exchange words, there was no need.

Atalasian offered Tahira a pine tea and toasted her health. "You should be aware that I am extremely angry with you for jumping off the cart, I was going to execute the driver until he convinced me that you made him swear an oath." He paused, "You know we came looking for you, every day, several times a day."

Tahira reached over and touched his arm. "There was no other option my friend, your people need you and, Matai needs you, I had to buy you time, and judging by this glorious city it was the right thing to do."

Atalasian shook his head. He knew she spoke the truth. A woman wise beyond her years had taught him a valuable lesson and he was grateful for it. "So what happened? We remained safe in our mountain hideaway for a couple of days. Once we came to realise that Dogon was no longer coming for us we sent scouts out to search for you. We had people stay in the village in the hope that you would find your way there. My spy in the Dogon camp confirmed that no one with light skin had been found or killed. We sent people out further and further. We even searched the rocky outcrop overlooking the great plains of the Dogon people, still no sign of them or, more importantly, you, for seven days and seven nights we have searched for you, we thought you were gone."

Once more Tahira was faced with a dilemma. No one would believe what she had done. Even she had trouble accepting that she was capable of the things she was able to do. "Well I'll be honest with you I don't think this is over. The Dogon will rise again." She sighed, at least that much was true. "Anyway, when I had been to the bluff before I had noticed some animals moving around at the base of the rocky ledge and I observed that there was quite a large area of land that they avoided, I rolled a boulder down and it lay on the surface for a few seconds before the ground swallowed it."

Matai, although tired, interrupted, "So let me guess, you used those flaming arrows of yours, or whatever you call them, to create a diversion and smokescreen so that they would stumble into the quicksand, you then pick off a few of their soldiers with your arrows to cause even more disarray, your enemy will then engage in internal fighting before retreating to lick their wounds, the old ruse of diversion and distraction eh?"

There was an audible intake of breath, Tahira smiled. Having Matai around certainly made life a little bit easier for her.

Matai continued, "When I was a slave I had witnessed this Celtic tactic, only it was so cold up there that they used bog lands instead of quicksand, " she let out a forced laugh, "Yep, it's classic military practice up there were those bloody heathens live." She coughed as she waved a finger vaguely in a northerly direction.

Atalasian needed no further invitation, "Please Tahira, what are these flaming arrows my love speaks of?"

"Right outside everyone, that's enough now, Matai needs her rest, go!" Amir was taking his role as court physician seriously and he answered to no one.

Reluctantly the group left with the King promising Tahira a full tour of the city in the morning. Elita placed her arm in Tahira's and showed her the way to their quarters.

"I'm going back to Aija tonight." Elita was apologetic but resolute, "my men have been left there for far too long, Atalasian has given me lots of supplies and goods to trade, we will head back to the land of the Ice and Snow before the sea freezes in the winter season, I would love for you to come and join us." Her words faded away. Her watery eyes were the sign that she knew the answer to that question before she asked it.

"Not this time my friend, I will however be here when you get back, and please bring back boxes and boxes of pine needles. You know how much I love my pine tea." Tahira smiled, saying goodbye was not going to be easy.

As night descended the camel train bound for the ship Aija was readied. They said their farewells. Just as Elita was about to mount her camel Tahira approached and gave her one final hug, "Look up at that star," Tahira pointed to the Great Dog constellation, "The brightest one you can see, if ever you get lonely, or need something, simply look up to that star and make a wish, you never know it might just hear you, it always makes me feel better anyway." As Elita looked to the star it seemed to brighten just a little.

Elita mustered a smile as she left with her guides. She had also asked Amir to come with her but he said his duty was to Matai, besides he preferred the warmth of sun, it reminded him of his own home.

The following morning Tahira visited her friend Matai. Her continued improvement was clear to see. Amir left the women alone.

TAHIRA THE ELEMENTAL

Matai was feeling emboldened, "So what did my little firestarter actual do, did you set them all aflame?"

Tahira looked slightly embarrassed, "I didn't, I couldn't, there were thousands of them," she paused briefly, "It was pretty much as you suggested, I set off lots of little fires, created lots of smoke to add to the confusion and a lot of them wandered into the quicksand, and they just, you know, gave up."

Matai gave her a knowing look, "My dear Tahira, there are lots of things I don't know but don't forget I grew up a Dogon, I know my father's lands like the back of my hand, there is no quicksand, sorry, there 'was' no quicksand." She raised her hand to stop Tahira speaking, "Look, I know you are a gifted young lady and, I am grateful to you, as I know Atalasian is, but promise me that you are OK and that you'll never do something as risky again, you have got the whole of your life ahead of you, remember?"

Tahira avowed that she was feeling good. In fact she couldn't think of a time when she had felt better. She deliberately avoided the second part of Matai's question and quickly changed the subject, "So tell me, what happened to you?"

"Oh they got lucky, if I had seen them I would have killed them but." She involuntarily touched the scar on the back on her skull. Although her short cropped hair was starting to grow back Amir had shaved it completely to keep the wound clean. "I woke up tied to a camel, I knew he was one of my people and I demanded I speak with my father, it didn't go well!" She took a sip of her pine tea, "At first he didn't believe it was me, he began to auction me off, a wife to the highest bidder. I spoke my mother's name, I then turned to Adeveima and called out her bastard son's name Yurugobi and told her about how much pleasure it gave me to have killed him. I don't really remember much else, my father's rage overtook him and he beat me, in front of his clan he beat his only surviving daughter to within an inch of her life, if I could have freed my hands I would have killed him." Tahira could see the fire in her eyes, and had no doubt as to the truth of her statement, "And that is it, I don't recall anything else until I came too after the first night in the mountains." She paused as a single tear fell from her cheek, Tahira felt her pain. "You know, if you had killed them all, I am not sure that I would feel sorry for them, they are my people no more."

They sat in silence for little while until Tahira subconsciously played with her amulet. Matai noted that one of the quarters now had a green crystal in it. "So have you been treating yourself my young friend?"

Tahira quickly dismissed the idea, "No, nothing like that at all, I wouldn't even know where to begin, it was like this after I had my long sleep, it is pretty though!" Matai reached out to touch it. It felt warm. "Anyway, let's talk about you." She placed her hand on Matai's stomach, "It's just as well you're your father concentrated his anger on your head and not on the rest of your body." Matai looked confused, "Someone didn't take her 'magic potion' before, or after, meeting our lovely King Atalasian did they?" She paused briefly, "You can close your mouth now, it's not very lady like."

Amir arrived with the Atlantean king and ushered both him and Tahira away.

TAHIRA THE ELEMENTAL

"It would appear my Lord Atalasian that now would be a good time for you to tell me all about this new city of yours." Tahira grabbed the King's arm and led him out of his own house as Matai waved his concerns away.

He led her to an imposing large black basalt walled building, a short distance away, "This is our council meeting place." Clearly brimming with pride he spread out a large piece of papyrus across a table. It was a map, "This place is the long dead centre of an old volcano, I found this many years ago while out hunting, I wanted somewhere safe for my people so ten or eleven years ago we started executing our plans, look there," his finger pointed to the entrance of the mountain pass she had come along the previous day, "this was a small ravine that we widened enough to get a cart through, we used the stone to make the gatehouses, and look there," he pointed to another entrance on the opposite side of the map, "this is another entrance/exit that we made, it leads to the great lake." Tahira followed as Atalasian made his way out of the building and on to one of the four straight roads that divided the city of Atlassia into quarters.

As they walked Tahira listened intently to the king. He went to great lengths to explain the structure of the city. It was approximately two miles across and was roughly circular in shape. The black stone government buildings, the great library and the amphitheatre with its stunning cupola roof made from sun baked earth and clay tiles where located around a small central plaza. The remaining civic buildings surrounded these with the citizen's stone houses radiating out from that central point. It reminded her of a series of rings gradually getting bigger. The farmers and their properties where positioned nearer the edge and contained within the parcel of land that they worked. The King explained how they had collected the extremely fertile volcanic ash from near the lake shore, and, deposited it on the city outskirts creating the lush farmland they could see before them.

Water was collected from the steep sides of the caldera and through a series of cut channels and drains irrigated the farmer's fields. It also provided the city's drinking water through a network of hand pumps spread throughout the complex. They were able to provide all the food, and more, for the whole community from within the city walls. Atalasian was excited about the possibility of being able to trade their surplus produce with other peoples. He went on to explain that now that they felt safer they would begin the next phase of development. He described how they would build a stone jetty to operate as a dock. They would be able to trade with the other kingdoms based around the great lake, once they had built some ships of course!

"So why where you still living in the settlement with your mud huts and fences made from dried wood?" Tahira was in awe of what she had seen. Even the wealthiest of the Celtic noblemen couldn't do what Atalasian had done.

He smiled, ever the diplomat, "Simple really, since time began my people have been nomads. With every season we would move to better grazing for our animals, or for better hunting or access to clean water. The idea of staying in one fixed place went against our historic way of living, a few of the more adventurous families came here as an experiment and loved it. They learned how to quarry stone. The houses they built where stronger and warmer. They were able to grow plenty of food. They found large pockets of obsidian glass from which we made our beads. Even the clay we use for our pots comes from near here. It was these forerunners that learned how to make the roofing tiles you see all around us." He paused briefly, "Gradually more and more of the younger people came and settled here. They began to bring their goods back to our settlement and set up the market that you have seen previously. But even with all these achievements still many hundreds of my people resisted. People fear change. They become comfortable with what they know. Many times I heard my tribes people complain to my councillors about how there is no need to fix something that isn't broken."

"So let me guess, the threat of war from your Dogon neighbours finally convinced them to move?" Tahira took a moment to look around her. Atlassia was a bustling, vibrant place with an energy that she found intoxicating.

"Ultimately yes but, to be fair the die had been cast over two years ago. We experienced a major drought which devastated the lands all around us for hundreds of miles. Several tribes were almost wiped out, such was the catastrophe, and yet we were the only tribe in the area whose watering hole didn't run dry. Other tribes learned of our good fortune and started helping themselves. To begin with it wasn't much of a problem but then they began to get greedy, particularly the Dogon. Despite our complaints they continued and threatened my people if they denied them access. They knew they were stronger and that we couldn't afford a confrontation. Within weeks it was gone. Even now after a couple of wet seasons it remains dry." He turned his gaze up towards the surrounding mountain tops, "Now, as you can see the very tops of these mountains are almost always shrouded in mists and cloud providing us with a constant supply of fresh clean drinking water. So we were able to survive although all the water has to be brought to the settlement. This however did not go unnoticed by the Dogon and they obviously tried to find out our new source. Fortunately the rains came however and, they lost interest, but we learned a valuable lesson and my people finally accepted that it was purely a matter of time before we relocated to our city in the mountains, and our new home, Atlassia."

Tahira knew that inside he was bursting with pride and so he should be. She had to accept that this place beautiful, almost magical. Everyone she saw had a smile of their faces, they seemed healthy and their children happy.

"Obviously once we realised that war was imminent there was no other option. Amastan, the goat herder who brought you here was the last stubborn old fool to resist but his wife, Kahina, liked having water readily available." He tapped the side of his nose, "Although, I suspect she particularly enjoys our bath house. I mean who doesn't enjoy a nice warm bath chatting with friends." He laughed as he rolled up the map.

"What's a, bath house, my dear Atalasian?"

The King smiled, "Think of it as a small pool filled with warm water. It's a place where you can wash your hair and your body. Now think of sharing it with some friends over a glass of wine or two and that's your bath house. Obviously there is one for the men and a separate one for you women."

Tahira made a mental note to try a warm bath later as it had to be better than the quick dip in freezing cold water that she was used too.

TAHIRA THE ELEMENTAL

Having completed the initial tour they had made their way back to the main central plaza. One of the King's councillors approached. "My Lord, can I disturb you for one moment please?" Atalasian nodded, "Sire, I have drawn up this afternoon's proclamation and I just wanted to confirm with you that all children aged between four and fourteen are to be sent to school every morning for five days a week, including the girls?" Once more Atalasian nodded, "But, what if they refuse?"

The king visibly bristled, "As I said in last night's council meeting it is through education and only education, that our society will evolve, in generations to come the Atlantean people will be revered throughout the known world as masters of science, philosophy, art and military defence, anyone who denies their child this opportunity will be given one demerit for each day of non-attendance. And, when we celebrate our annual harvest and award every person their share of the profits we will deduct from that any demerits that they have accumulated throughout the previous year." He took a breath before continuing, "Look, I am aware that this is new to people but I want to take the old burden of educating our children away from the families themselves. Eventually all our teachers will be fully trained across all subjects but for now we will rely on volunteers to impart such wisdom as they have. One teacher can teach twenty or thirty children at a time and therefore free up the parents to work elsewhere."

"You can also tell them that Tahira will be one of their teachers and I will take it personally if they don't turn up for school." The aide nervously glanced at Atalasian before hurrying away. The King laughed loudly.

"Are you sure my dear Tahira? Come with me, I'll show you to your new home." The ruler of the Atlantean people strode confidently away catching Tahira by surprise. She had to run to catch up.

She recognised the library from the map she had seen earlier. The building next to it was to be her new work place. This school house was set in its own area. There was a large field, presumably for athletics and other games. She could also see other supplementary buildings within the compound.

Atalasian made his excuses as he needed to talk to his chief engineer about building a hospital now that Amir had accepted the role of Chief Physician.

Tahira spent the afternoon preparing for the days ahead as best as she could. She had surprised herself by volunteering to teach. She wasn't normally an impulsive person but it felt right, somehow. She wasn't sure how, or what, to teach but whatever she did impart, it would be through fun. She had been taught so many things by her father, and her inner voice, it seemed only right and proper to share that gained knowledge.

In the early evening she made her way to the female bath house which was several hundred paces away from the men's.

At first she was uncomfortable about disrobing in front of the other women but no one else seemed to be bothered. She let the warm water cover the whole of her body so that only her head remained dry. The other women kept themselves to themselves. Tahira heard them discuss the events of their day. Others complained about their respective husbands. Some gossiped about their neighbours. There was even some muted laughter. But no one would dare look at the fair skinned woman who had single-handedly defeated the might of the

TAHIRA THE ELEMENTAL

Dogon tribe. Tahira wanted to talk to them. She wanted them to see that she was just like them in so many ways. Just then Kahina came in and immediately sat next to Tahira. She smiled and offered to wash Tahira's hair for her. The clay bar she used had been infused with oil from the Argan tree and various ground spices. The smell was intoxicating. One of the other women now approached to help dry her hair and then plait it. It occurred to Tahira that it wasn't just the colour of her skin that differentiated her from the native Atlantean people. Her long flowing auburn hair had also set her apart. She was unsure as to how long she had spent in the bath house but by the time she got back to her schoolhouse the need for sleep had overtaken her.

For the first time since arriving at the mountain hideaway Matai was out of bed and shooing Amir away when Tahira paid her friend a visit. Amir was not to be out done and wouldn't leave until she had taken her medicine.

Tahira wanted to tell Matai her news but Matai already knew. Tahira suspected that she had been the willing 'victim' of a plot hatched by Matai and Atalasian. She left smiling and grabbed Amir by the arm leading him out of the house.

"So Amir, what do I call you now, The Court Physician, The Healing Master?"

Amir knew he was being teased, "Well the 'school mistress' can call me The Great One, it's got a nice ring to it don't you think?"

"Well I am honoured that, The Great One, does deem it fit to allow a poor, lowly servant girl to be seen in his esteemed company." She kissed him on the cheek, "Alas I must go, Oh Great One." She curtsied before running off.

Amir vowed that he would never wash that part of his face again, well not until later that evening in the bath house. Still feeling elated he turned down one of the flag stoned streets to meet up with the civil engineer who was going to build him his hospital.

It was only the second day since she had arrived at the great city of Atlassia but here she was standing in front of a full classroom of wide eyed children. They were excited, some had even washed. After taking a register of names they began their lessons. She was pleased to see Kahina and Lunja and even more delighted to learn that Kahina had volunteered as a teacher. Another volunteer came in the shape of Jamilah, the mother of one of the youngest children. She was in her mid-twenties and the wife of Chike, who was the youngest member of Atalasian's council of advisors.

As lunchtime approached and therefore the end of the teaching day Tahira had allotted time for stories. The children took the opportunity to ask all about Tahira, where she was from, her adventures and how she defeated the whole of the Dogon tribe. But what they really wanted to know was, could she do magic?

Smiling and with great patience Tahira recounted her journey missing lots of the more gruesome details of course. She told tales of escaping injustice, of pirate adventures on the high seas, of exploring new lands and of how friendship and love are the greatest gifts of all.

The children went home at bit later than expected but smiling and feeling blessed. Jamilah watched and observed. This young woman from another land was truly magical.

TAHIRA THE ELEMENTAL

Tahira's life began to settle into a routine. Each night she dreamt of science, philosophy and the arts. Each morning she revealed the secrets of her dreams to her attentive young audience. Kahina and Jamilah also blossomed into their roles. Amir became a regular visitor to the school both during lessons but also after the school had closed for the day.

Within a couple of weeks Matai was fully recovered and assisting Atalasian with his civic duties. Even though her days were busy there was always time for afternoon pine tea with her best friend Tahira before heading off for the daily bath ritual with the other ladies.

After a few months the bump in Matai's tummy was pronounced enough that she could no longer deny the cause. She agreed to be Atlassia's queen which resulted in a three day celebratory party.

Amir's small but expandable hospital was opened. There were few patients requiring his care, so he spent quite a lot of time writing a papyrus book of medicinal treatments for common ailments.

Within three months trade routes had been set up across the great lake, and soon the city was being visited by leading dignitaries from other civilisations. They were all impressed and in awe of the Atlantean achievements. Some sent scholars, some sent merchants but they all looked upon this great city with envious eyes. They wanted to learn its secrets, its strengths but more importantly its weaknesses.

The Queen of Persea

Matai and Atalasian welcomed their son, Abidemi into the world on the first day of their wet season. He wasn't aware of how much the city of his birth had grown and developed over his gestation period.

His arrival coincided with his tribe's harvest celebrations and meant that the Atlantean people welcomed more guests than ever before. Many brought gifts but none were more treasured than the boxes of pine needles that Elita brought back with her from her trading mission with her own people. The supply of pine tea had all but run out. Tahira was only too pleased to show Elita around the magnificent city she now called home.

It took several days before the city returned to its normal state. The people returned to their jobs as the various important dignitaries returned to their home lands.

After school one afternoon Elita paid a visit to Tahira. It was the first opportunity since she had arrived to speak with her friend privately. She watched and gave a knowing look to Tahira as Amir made his excuses and left. He wanted to check up on Abidemi, although his primary reason was to try and get Matai to rest but she was being resistant!

It was no secret that Tahira and Amir were together and had been for several months. Elita was happy for them both but Tahira knew that there was a purpose to her friend's visit.

She decided to start on a lighter note, "So did you meet up with your family?"

"Aye, all is good, it had been three years since I ran away, my father is still very much in charge and still wanting to marry me off to some other clan chief, he still treats my Mother like a dog at times but at least she was pleased to see me."

"Did he say much when he saw The Happy Falcon?"

"Well he offered to buy Aija from me because she is fast and well built, but, when I refused he said he didn't want it anyway. My mother told me that he was in fact very proud of what I had done but could never admit it to me or to my elder brothers. Just the usual stuff really." She paused briefly, "Unfortunately, where I come from women are treated very much inferior to men so I am not the most popular person to have around." She laughed, "Anyway I have made my peace with it, I will visit as a trader but, Aija is my home now."

"I am so sorry for you." Tahira reached to hold her friends hand.

"Thank you Tahira but there is no need, I have the life that I want and I am no longer a slave, either to a certain Captain Felix, or to my father and his clan."

"So what of other news? Judging by you clothes you are becoming successful as a merchant."

"Business is good. Most traders aren't used to dealing with a female captain. I sometimes catch them ogling me and use it to my advantage, especially the married ones who are frightened of their wives." Once more she threw her head back and laughed. Tahira suspected there were more tales to be told but Elita quickly returned to a more serious tone, "Unfortunately the various tribes of Celta are at war with each other. King Alba and his troops are gradually moving to the southern part of the island. He is enslaving other clans and executing anyone who opposes him. It's forced the Franecian slavers to abandon their Celta raiding parties and look for new opportunities including Juteria."

"What about your family, are they safe?"

"For now yes, winter is coming and with it the strong northerly winds. The resultant storms will keep us safe from their opportunistic raids. It won't however protect us from the heathens from the east, if the rumours are true. Apparently they are amassing their troops and looking to expand into the west and Juteria may be a target. I tell you Tahira this world is becoming a more dangerous place to live, unlike here of course." She smiled and changed the subject, "I never imagined you as a teacher"

"Neither did I my friend, neither did I."

• • • •

Amir was attending Queen Matai and Abidemi when, from an adjoining corridor, he heard a language he had not heard spoken for many years.

He went to investigate. He saw a rather small dishevelled man admonishing two servants who were fidgeting nervously. The corridor led to Atalasian's state room where he would regularly meet representatives and diplomats from other cultures. Amir introduced himself in the man's own language, he was clearly shocked. He quickly composed himself however and returned the greeting just as the door opened. He apologised to Amir, they had been granted a brief audience with the King of the Atlantean people and didn't want to miss their appointment.

Amir enjoyed a level of freedom around the court and followed them in. He formally bowed to the King before joining the other aides off to the side of the throne. Amir knew that this state room had been built for show. It had an impressive façade showcasing the artisan skills of the Atlantean people. It was a display of wealth and power for the whole world to see. He reflected that only a year ago they had projected a very different face to their neighbouring countries, with their wealth and skills being carefully hidden under a façade of mud huts and stifling traditions. It was as if the arrival of Matai had lifted an oppressive cloud off Atalasian's shoulders. He had a vision for what the future of his people could be and was both proud and determined to show it to the world.

Amir smiled as he reminded himself that Atalasian was actually a very approachable ruler who would regularly visit his people and take tea with them. But that's not how the outside world saw him. Other kingdoms were built on fear and intimidation. They simply assumed that that was how Atalasian achieved his success. To him the idea that the king of the Atlanteans was an all-powerful and all conquering leader was laughable.

The slightly bedraggled envoy introduced himself and his people. His name was Sadiri a humble servant to Queen Makida from the land of the Persean's. He was clearly troubled with speaking the universal language of commerce and trade. He stumbled and stuttered his way through a series of proclamations wishing King Atalasian and his people great fortune and happiness.

TAHIRA THE ELEMENTAL

Atalasian had not been sleeping well since the birth of his son. He did his best to hide this fact but found himself interrupting Sadiri on multiple occasions in his desire to try and speed the process up. He had long decided that being a King had some downsides to it. Sadiri became less confident and more nervous at each interjection. He clearly had memorised a script and was determined to get through it as best he could.

Amir recognised that the King was about to dismiss Sadiri. He came out from the shadow of the King's retinue and after formally bowing to the King he offered to help. The King was only too glad to have his offer of assistance.

Amir turned to Sadiri and once more spoke in the Persean language. "King Atalasian is honoured to have received your Queen's greetings and sincerest best wishes." Sadiri nodded as Amir translated what he had just said to the Lion King. Not being an astute diplomat Amir simply asked, "And may we enquire as to what it is it your Queen desires from the Atlantean people?"

Sadiri was slightly taken aback by Amir's impertinence but quickly composed himself, "My people are but poor, uneducated farmers."

Amir snorted in derision and quickly interrupted him, "I am proud to call myself a Persean." he involuntarily puffed out his chest, "We are neither poor nor uneducated, only the lazy and ignorant attest to your remark."

The diplomat bowed even lower, "Sir, please forgive me, I mean no offense. It is true that until recently we enjoyed a better level of fortune but these last few years, since the major drought, have seen us endure a terrible famine. We are also subject to outbreaks of disease." He turned to face Atalasian, "Oh gracious and wise one, my Queen simply asks, no, begs for your help." He waited for Amir to translate.

This intervention intrigued the King, they had never been asked for help before. He waved his hand, indicating his desire for Sadiri to continue.

Without averting his eyes, Sadiri continued, "My Queen has heard about the skills of the Atlantean people particularly in the field of medicine and civil engineering." He took a deep breath, "She would be eternally grateful to you if you would do her the honour of visiting her and bringing some of your experts so that we may learn from them."

Amir translated the request but struggled to hide his contempt. He didn't wait for Atalasian's reply before turning back to Sadiri and reverting back to his native tongue, "Why would we help? You have the great Court Physician Zawahi at your disposal do you not? Besides I have never heard of Queen Makida so why should we help you?"

Sadiri looked puzzled but before he could respond King Atalasian raised his hand, "Amir, I am struggling with this would you therefore be kind enough to spend some time with our guest and come back with their actual request so I can make an informed decision." The King quickly dismissed them doing his utmost to stifle a yawn.

Refreshments were brought to a small anteroom just off the corridor.

"You introduced yourself as Amir, that is a Persean name and you speak our language. May I ask?"

Amir didn't wait for Sadiri to finish, "My father, may he rest in peace, was called Airyaman." He waited for some recognition but it didn't come, "He was Court Physician to the Great King Tudiya."

"Ah, King Tudiya." Sadiri seemed wistful, "Well my dear Amir it is I that owe you an explanation, you see, I have only recently been brought into the court of Queen Makida, less than two seasons, so my knowledge of old diplomatic events is somewhat limited. Sadly I have not heard of your Father so please forgive me for that, I am sure that he was a great man." Amir nodded his acceptance, "Clearly though you have knowledge of the court so please allow me to bring you up to date, how long have you been away?"

"It's been nearly five years since I left, my father had died four years before when I was ten. With King Tudiya's blessing my Mother, Thriti, apprenticed me to the great Zawahi." Sarcasm dripped from his voice, "he was a drunk and a bully and after my mother passed I ran away before being captured and enslaved by the heathens from the north." Amir was visibly upset at the memory.

Ever the diplomat, Sadiri paused briefly before speaking, "Let us start there then, if I may? King Tudiya was a wise man and appreciated beautiful things, after his wife had died in child birth many years ago he took a vow never to remarry, he was devoted to his son Tudizade, you may remember him." Amir hadn't heard that name in a long time. They were of similar ages but he had little memory of ever seeing him. "Sadly, Tudizade died four years ago, the King was distraught and locked himself away. He forgot to rule the people and the land. The rains never came and we experienced our first famine in a lifetime, eventually his councillors persuaded him to help his people before it was too late. At the same time a noble from the southern coastal lands came to court with his young wife, Makida, asking for help. The King fell under her spell and after her husband suddenly passed away they were married. Our Oracles predicted the birth of a great Kingdom, the people celebrated."

"So what happened?"

"My understanding is that things were well to begin with. However, the King was already an old man and, more than twice the age of Makida. He died within six months of their union and without an heir Queen Makida took control. Sadly the unknown disease that had killed the King also took out nearly all the court. Only the Queen and her closest friends survived unscathed, your Zawahi could do nothing, in fact he was found guilty of negligence and executed, and then last year the crops failed and we had another famine. We had plenty of water in the mountains but no way of getting it to our fields. " His voice trailed off.

Amir swallowed hard. This was completely unexpected news. He mentioned a few names from court that he could remember. Sadiri confirmed that none of those people where still around, they would either be dead or in self-imposed exile.

Sadiri brought the conversation back around as to why they needed King Atalasian's help. "We are unable to offer any treasures for your peoples help. Queen Makida however assures the King of her unfailing commitment as a loyal and trusted ally."

The King and his councillors reconvened to hear the results of Amir's conversation with Queen Makida's envoy. One aide was firm, "I don't like it your majesty." Another commented, "It is but a trap my Lord." Others argued that it might be good for future trade and that they should send a delegation instead, but this was quickly dismissed.

Atalasian duly considered the varied options that his people laid before him. As the King rose to his feet the discussion ceased. "Having heard all the arguments please convey to Sadiri that due to my commitments here that I am unable to accept Queen Makida's kind invitation. We understand that this decision is not what the people of Persea want to hear. We will however provide three ships full of medicine and food as a gesture of good will and will look to provide more help in the future."

There was a general murmur of agreement. "I'll go." Amir's voice was unexpectedly soft and barely above a whisper.

King Atalasian stopped in his tracks and turned to face his young friend. "Amir, you surprise me, what about your duties?"

"But my Lord, whilst this is my home they are my people. If it is as bad as they say then I am more than qualified to help, my duties here are light and can be managed by the nurses that I have trained here, if I get this right then we shall have a friend for life and others will look favourably on us for doing this."

The king reached out his hand to shake Amir's, "Then go with my blessing my friend."

Amir arrived back at the schoolhouse just as Tahira and Elita were returning from the bathhouse.

"Hey Amir, you need to say goodbye to Elita, she's off in the morning, we won't see her until next summer." Tahira was trying to put a brave face on it. Her friend had only been there for a short while and she was going to miss her.

Amir wished her good luck and looked forward to seeing her soon. But Tahira noted something in his manner. She waited until Elita had left.

"Why the long face Mister?" Tahira hoped that her upbeat tone might induce a smile from Amir, it didn't.

He held her hand as he talked her through the events of his day, "Then I will come with you, we are partners after all!" Tahira was adamant. Amir tried to talk her out if it. It would be a long journey. She was needed here, what about her friends?

Tahira waved away his concerns, she was coming with him whether he liked it or not! Amir had secretly hoped that Tahira would offer to come with him. He had long accepted that he would be lost without the woman he loved.

They said goodbye to Elita the following morning and began making their preparations for their journey to Persea. The Persean envoy also left with his small retinue. Sadiri wanted to inform his Queen so that they could make preparations.

It took a couple of days to fully load the small flat bottomed Atlantean designed boats. They had living quarters in the bow end and were powered by a single sail. Although the inland lake, Mediati, was vast, it was also very shallow. In fact huge areas of the lake bed would be exposed in the heat of the summer. The visible mud flats would crack horizontally allowing you to peel the clay off the surface. When reconstituted with water it was their main source of material to make their cooking pots from.

The southern section of Lake Mediati was the most prone to the effects of drought however given that winter had just arrived they expected to make steady albeit slow progress.

TAHIRA THE ELEMENTAL

Although, at first reluctant to take on the school teaching fully, Jamilah, and Kahina promised to make sure that the children continued to have fun learning in Tahira's absence. Although they confessed that the weekly archery practice would be put on hold for fear of losing a child or two.

King Atlassia and his consort Queen Matai came to bid them farewell and a safe journey. Matai was a little envious of the adventure but looking into the eyes of her baby son she knew that she needed to remain. She and Abidemi did walk as high as they could up the mountains to keep watch on the three little ships as they sailed off into the distance.

Sadiri had left instructions to simply hug the south coast of the lake. After a few days you would see the Persean capital city of Susa. It was impossible to miss.

With little to do, their time was spent in conversation, playing games or simply staring out at the vast waterway. Amir taught Tahira some words and phrases in his native tongue. With her gift for languages she quickly was able to converse like a local. "You are a truly gifted woman." Amir kissed her.

Tahira shrugged her shoulders, "Just lucky I guess." She had never spoken to Amir about her inner voice and the help it provided. He had often asked about her multi-coloured amulet but she had simply waved it off as a gift from her unknown mother. Not even Matai knew the full truth of her ability.

Sadiri was waiting on the quayside as they docked. "Please come with me, Queen Makida is looking forward to meeting you my Lord Amir." Tahira shot a quick glance towards Amir, he was slightly embarrassed but said nothing.

Amir breathed in the city air. He hadn't realised that he was so close to home. The mud brick houses, the noise even the smell of the spices used in Persean cooking was all so familiar to him.

The sprawling metropolis of Susa the capital of Persea was impressive. There were lots of people milling around, it looked busy. They made their way along the main street leading to a large palace at the top of a small hill.

Whilst Amir was comfortable in his surroundings, Tahira was not. Her intuition told her to be wary. She had expected it to be somewhat smaller, more impoverished. They had been told the people were starving and disease ridden. She felt that they were being watched by unseen eyes. Lost in her thoughts she almost walked into the back of Amir as they had come to a sudden stop at the palace gates.

The grand ceremonial palace was a large complex. There were natural and man-made terraces. Each terrace was split by a single large stone staircase flanked by ornately carved stone balustrades. On either side each terrace had a range of small buildings. The third terrace was the high point of the complex and the final destination of the central stairway. It led to two large wooden doors at least the height of two men. They were heavily carved with a relief which appeared to depict previous battles and victories.

At the top of the stairs was a walkway that flowed around the central building. Its roof supported by white marble columns. This was the same material used on the walls of the palace. There were no windows and the glare from the sunlight reflecting off the marble gave it a bedazzling appearance. Tahira had a quick glance behind her expecting to see the city below but the view was blocked by the high, thick stone wall that surrounded the citadel. She caught a glimpse of a guard casually patrolling along the top of the wall.

Sadiri raised his black wooden staff and with great ceremony struck the heavily ornate teak doors. With a large amount of effort the doors creaked and groaned as they opened from the inside. They walked forward with Amir leading the way. His chest puffed out he wanted to present a show of confidence. As Tahira followed the two guards crossed their spears in front of her.

Sadiri was slightly condescending, "My sincere apologies Mistress Tahira, concubines are not allowed in the palace itself, Queen Makida will see Lord Amir alone."

"Then I shall not be meeting with your Queen either, please convey our sincerest apologies for any misunderstanding." Amir had seen the look of disgust on Tahira's face and had sought to defuse the situation. They turned away as Sadiri, grovelling, hurriedly entered the throne room.

As they reached the top of the stairs they were once more confronted by the two guards who blocked their way.

"My honoured guests of Atlantea, please forgive me and our, old fashioned ways." Looking back through the double doors Queen Makida was calling to them. She was moving quickly with the subordinate Sadiri at her heel. "We are but simple people and our customs and practices are I fear, somewhat dated." She bowed her head as she shook their hands, "Come let us take tea in less formal surroundings."

If the queen's behaviour was unfamiliar to her people then they did not show it. As she walked the gallery with her small party in tow her people bowed and curtsied almost prostrating themselves on the floor. No one looked her in the eyes.

They arrived at a small ante room off to the left hand side of the palace building itself. "Please do come in, these are my private quarters."

She sat down at the end of a solidly built but plain teak table and invited her guests to follow suit. Sadiri clapped his hands and within seconds Tahira and Amir were each presented with a small glass filled with hot aromatic black tea. Amir formally bowed his head at his host before taking a sip. Tahira repeated his gesture. She was still fuming inside. Amir knew he was going to have to do some explaining later.

Tahira listened without saying much as Amir engaged in conversation with Queen Makida and her aide. He informed her that King Atalasian welcomed contact with the Persean people and was apologetic that his stately duties prevented him from attending in person. For her part Queen Makida was grateful for the help that the Atlantean people had offered her people.

"So I understand that you are a schoolteacher." Tahira was caught off guard by Queen Makida's direct approach to her. She politely nodded, "Is it common in Atlantea for women of low status to marry above their station?" Queen Makida smiled.

"We're not married your majesty." Tahira was composed but could feel the anger well inside her.

"Not now my child, not now."

"Oh, interesting! I clearly have got so much to learn about your way of doing things, maybe you could be my schoolteacher?" Queen Makida rose. The meeting was over.

TAHIRA THE ELEMENTAL

Sadiri showed their guests to their quarters. It was no coincidence that Amir and Tahira where given Zawahi's old rooms. The previous Court Physician had amassed a large collection of various potions, tinctures and poultices. Some he was familiar with and others not. They were still in the main laboratory that Amir had spent much of his early teenage years in.

Tahira was pacing up and down with her arms crossed. Amir tried to reassure her, "Look, our society is not much different to lots of others. Men are the workers, the politicians and the fighters. The women are the homemakers and mothers. It's not right, believe me I get it, but look they do have a Queen in charge and that's a start at least, isn't it?"

"Why didn't you tell me a bit more about, your way? Don't forget I grew up a slave. I know what is like to be some sort of play thing for some rich and powerful man." Tahira's words dripped with venom.

"To be honest, I had forgotten, I haven't been here for several years and my most recent experiences have been watching you, Matai and Elita, I certainly don't see women as being somehow 'beneath' men, I love you and we are partners, isn't that more important?"

Tahira knew that he was arguing from the perspective of privilege but, he had been a slave too. She decided that it was best to let it go, for now. "So tell me about the palace and the beautiful Queen Makida."

Amir inwardly acknowledged that Queen Makida was a woman of rare beauty. She would have been a few years older than him with long jet black hair. Her eyes were blue and rare for his people. A man could get lost in those eyes. He decided not to convey his thoughts to Tahira on that subject. "I only know what Sadiri told me and as to her beauty, I hadn't noticed but, now that you mention it, I would imagine that other people would agree with you but we are not here to judge, we have work to do."

He went on to explain that when he was a child he lived in the very house that they now occupied with his parents. A woman's role in Persean society clearly being different meant that they were forced to leave the palace estate after his father died. The Court Physician's house was then given to Zawahi to whom he was apprenticed. He was not allowed to go to the palace itself, nor was he allowed to engage with any member of the Royal family or adult palace officials. Although he did remember that his mother would sometimes be called upon to visit King Tudiya. Rumour had it that the floor of the inner palace hall where guests were introduced to the king was so shiny that it looked like the surface of the great lake.

Sadiri arrived in the morning. He advised them that the dock workers had completed the unloading of the food and medicines from their ship. Horses and carts were already leaving Susa with the food to be distributed to the needy. It would be sent to various outlying villages.

"Could we go and assist? I'm sure more hands would make light work." Tahira had decided that she needed to get away from the palace.

"There is absolutely no need, but thank you, the people of Persea will honour the people of Atlantean for their gift." Sadiri bowed, "Queen Makida would like to discuss the creation of a hospital with Lord Amir, in private of course. Lady Tahira, I could arrange for one of our women to show you around our lovely city, we don't have much to entertain someone as learned as yourself but you may find some things to interest you."

Amir had already collected a few things. Tahira felt that she had been outflanked, "Well how could I possibly reject such a kind offer." Tahira's voice dripped with sarcasm. Sadiri smiled as he left closely followed by Amir.

Amir entered the palace for the first time in his life. He was impressed. The floor of the great hall was as highly polished as the rumours had suggested. It was surprising reflective, like looking into a still clear water pond. What also surprised him was as he bowed in front of his Queen he could see underneath her regal robes.

Queen Makida smiled, "Please my Lord Amir take a seat."

Amir did as he was bid and laid his papyrus and drawings out in front of the Queen, "My Queen I have taken the liberty of making a few plans for you to review."

Queen Makida reached out and placed her hand gently on top of Amir's, "All in due course my dear Lord Amir, but first, please, tell me about the wonderful City of Atlassia. Are all the men as handsome as you?"

• • • •

Jasmina was of similar age to Tahira. She worked in the palace kitchen but lived in the city of Susa itself. She had volunteered to be Lady Tahira's guide for the day as it was better than washing dishes and fending off some of the more lascivious men of the court.

Tahira was enjoying a cup of pine tea that she had brought with her. She found the Persian black tea too bitter. She was sitting on a small terrace outside of their guest lodgings when Jasmina was introduced to her.

Jasmina had expected to meet a grand older lady. She was even more surprised when Tahira began speaking perfect Persean and offered her a pine tea. It's subtle and slightly sweet flavour reminded her of an upland forest she had visited as a child.

Whilst Jasmina felt awkward to begin with it didn't take long for Tahira's charms to win her over. Tahira for her part had warmed to her. Given that she did not expect to see Amir until the evening she agreed that maybe they should visit the town centre and take in the sights and sounds of the busy metropolis.

As they left the palace Jasmina covered her hair and mouth with a veil. Only her gorgeous dark orangey-brown eyes were visible. She offered a veil to Tahira who was reluctant to wear it.

"It is our custom, a woman who does not wear it is an 'outsider' and will be treated as such, you will not be allowed to visit certain places, and my people will be very unwillingly to talk to you." Jasmina was showing Tahira how to wear the veil, Tahira did not resist.

They walked the streets. People were busy. To Tahira it felt different from the previous day, yesterday the people kept their heads low and didn't look at you. But today the city felt alive.

They made their way to see the captain of the ship that had brought Tahira here from Atlassia. However he and the other ships had gone. They found an older man who looked official and he informed them that the ships had received orders to return home as the guests where going to be staying a while in Susa. Tahira was somewhat concerned not because they hadn't expected to stay for a while but more because she was confident that the ship's captain would have advised them directly if he was leaving.

As they made their way back to the palace, Jasmina stopped by her house and introduced Tahira to her aged mother. Her father had died many years ago in a war with the Dogon people from the south. The mere mention of their name sent a shiver down Tahira's spine.

Stepping back outside on the cobbled streets a merchant was selling fruit and vegetables from the back of his cart. It surprised Tahira given the supposed famine that the country was suffering from. He wasn't even particularly busy. Jasmina bought some vegetables for her mother whilst Tahira went to stroke the mane of the horse that was standing patiently waiting for its next piece of work.

"They are beautiful, and so different from the one's I know back home." Tahira's voice was slightly wistful.

"Oh this one's seen better days," said Jasmina, "Bit of an old boy this one I'm afraid."

"The one's we have are much bigger, maybe taller than a man and half as wide."

"Are you a Celt?" Jasmina asked with wide eyes, she had heard tales, possibly myths about the savages from the Celtic islands. She had to admit that it would make sense as Tahira had a much fairer complexion. Tahira nodded as Jasmina grabbed her hand, "Come on, this might interest you."

She led Tahira along a street that ran parallel to the palace compound. As they climbed to the top of a small hill, and with the city of Susa at their backs, they saw a large, well laid out park. At the far end was a collection of tents and wooden structures.

"This is our army training ground, look see the horses at the far side." Jasmina was pointing to a small group of sleek black horses galloping under the control of their riders. They watched as the horsemen reached what looked like straw men. Without changing pace they were able to throw spears at these targets. Even Tahira was impressed.

As Tahira focused she could see other men practising hand to hand combat. They had bronze swords and small round shields. Each wore a helmet made from bronze. She counted at least a hundred men.

"Would you like to ride one of them, I mean the horses." Jasmina blushed as Tahira raised an eyebrow in her direction. "There is a horse riding school nearby, we could go tomorrow, maybe, if I'm allowed."

Tahira smiled, "I would like that very much."

They made their way back to the palace. Tahira told Jasmina a little bit about her childhood. She spoke about being enslaved and about how she managed to escape with the help of her friend Matai. Jasmina didn't need to know the details but it was nice to be able to tell her story. She was also glad to remove her veil as Jasmina went to continue her duties in the palace kitchen.

Amir arrived just before the evening meal. Tahira told him about her day and the concerns she had about their ship leaving unannounced. Amir seemed distant. He wasn't too bothered about the ship. However Queen Makida had signed off his plans for a new hospital in full. He was to start working on it straight away. Tahira was pleased to see the excitement in his face. He was doing a good thing. The success of his works in the city of Atlassia could be readily replicated here too.

The next day followed a similar pattern with Amir busy with the Queen and her council while Tahira was left to fend for herself. She was grateful that Jasmina had been given the role of Companion of our Honoured Guests. They laughed about how stupid a title it was but it beat working in the kitchens.

They visited the horse riding school. Tahira was amazed at how good a horsewoman Jasmina was. "My father was in the cavalry so maybe I just inherited his abilities." Jasmina beat Tahira in each of the 3 races they had, although Tahira was closing each time. The riding of these faster, smaller horses was different to her experience in Celta but she loved the speed and agility of these animals.

That evening Amir was more conversational. He still obsessed about his own work but listened more to Tahira. The next day however he was more reticent again.

"So how long do you think you need to be here?" As much as she enjoyed the company of Jasmina she had to confess that being a virtual prisoner in a foreign land was losing its appeal.

"Oh we'll be here for months at least." Amir then reeled off all the things he needed to get done, "And that's before we can take in any patients or begin training of the nurses etc."

"But they don't need you specifically to help with the building itself. They have got their own engineers and builders. We can come back in six months."

"You just don't get it do you!" Amir snapped before quickly realising his mistake, "Sorry, sorry, I shouldn't have shouted."

He calmed his voice down, "I'm just feeling the stress that's all. I really want this to work, for us and for our future, together!"

Tahira was shocked. She knew Amir had his faults, like everyone, but he had never raised his voice to her before.

He reached out to her and kissed away the single tear as it fell onto her cheek, he whispered, "I am so sorry my love! Please forgive me!" He now kissed her gently on the lips.

The next day Jasmina was not called for as Amir decided that they should spend the day together. Tahira quickly forgot the troubles of the previous evening. It was great to spend some time with the man she loved.

The following day Tahira had hoped to take Amir to the horse riding school but unfortunately for her Queen Makida had other ideas. Once more Jasmina was summoned to be Tahira's entertainment for the day whilst Amir regaled the Queen. That evening Amir made his excuses after their evening meal as he needed to work in his laboratory. Before going to bed Tahira took him a cup of pine tea but Amir barely looked up from his page of papyrus. He explained how he was busy working out the ingredients and the correct proportions for a new potion or something. She went to bed, Amir did not follow.

Tahira was surprised to find that not only was Amir not in their bed but that he had already left for work. A court official informed her that Queen Makida was meeting dignitaries from their north eastern Bysyrian neighbours and had requested Amir's attendance, he would be gone all day and possibly the evening as well.

Tahira spent the day with Jasmina. She tried to keep her spirits up but her mind constantly kept coming back to Amir.

TAHIRA THE ELEMENTAL

She loved him but, "Have you ever been in love Jasmina?" She asked coyly.

"Yes my lady, I have." Jasmina's normally bright optimistic voice now buckled. Raw emotion undercut the attempt of Jasmina to maintain her composure. "His name is Cyrus and he's a soldier. He is stationed somewhere along the border with the Dogon people. I miss him so much!" Instinctively Tahira held her companion.

Tahira lay awake for most of the night. She pretended to be asleep when Amir came home.

"Would you like to spend some time away from Susa, with me of course?" Amir caught Tahira by surprise.

"What, yes of course that would be wonderful? Are we going back to Atlassia?"

"No, why would I do that, no, Queen Makida," Tahira's heart sank at the mere mention of her name, "has asked me, along with Sadiri, to visit the Mycenean people. There is a potential war looming between them and the Bysyrians. Their visit today was to request Queen Makida's help to try and avert such a devastating conflict. She would go herself but has already promised to visit some of the drought affected lands further to the south of the country. She also wants to ensure that the building works for my hospital happen as planned."

"Oh Amir, this isn't what we signed up for."

"I know but, this is a great opportunity, imagine if we can prevent a war."

"But why you?"

"Well it was the Myceneans that first captured me after I ran away from Persea. I was enslaved by them for a whole winter season before being sold off, so I speak a little of their language and therefore a lot more than Sadiri does."

Tahira saw for the first time the gold seal ring that Amir wore. It glinted in the sunlight as Amir played with it, "It is Queen Makida's seal showing that I speak on her behalf."

"Sadiri doesn't have one."

"Yes, well Makida doesn't trust him as much."

"*He dropped the Queen from her name.*" She made a mental note. Tahira was unhappy with this turn of events but she also acknowledged that she needed to get away from this court. She hoped that it might do them both a bit of good.

"Ok." She said, "One condition, when it is done, we go home to Atlassia."

"Yes, absolutely, and one more thing, sorry but I need a favour from you, I promised Queen Makida that when we get back, and before we leave for Atlassia, that you would show her how you make, what do you call them, flaming arrows?"

Tahira was hesitant but agreed after all she had been teaching the people of Atlantea how to make and use them.

It was agreed that they would leave the next day. The quickest way to get there would be by ship to Mycenea's main port, Zakros. Amir left but promised he would be back before dark.

By midday Tahira had become increasingly concerned about her companion Jasmina. They had arranged the previous day to meet up to go horse riding. The palace kitchen staff confirmed that she was not due to work with them that day.

Putting on her veil Tahira left to visit her at home. Jasmina was distraught as her mother had passed away the previous night, not long after she had eaten her evening meal. Tahira stayed with her for the rest of the day and for the afternoon funeral. She was reluctant to leave her alone that evening and only did so on the assurance from Jasmina that she would be alright.

As Tahira walked through the door Amir began excitedly telling Tahira about the progress he'd made on a new potion to help people who suffer with seizures. It was fully five minutes before he realised that Tahira was not really listening to him, "What is up my love, are you not pleased?"

"Jasmina's mother passed away last night and we buried her this afternoon."

"Oh that is so sad, do they know what caused it?"

"No, as usual Jasmina took home some of the leftover food from the palace kitchen along with a small flagon of wine. Shortly after this her mother, who was sitting in a chair, simply closed her eyes, for the last time. Jasmina thought she had fallen asleep. She blames herself of course." Tahira was struggling to hold back the tears.

"Was it a small metal flagon made from bronze that is slightly more yellow than normal?"

"What a strange question, Amir, I have no idea, why does it matter?"

"Oh it doesn't matter at all. My love, it doesn't matter at all, shall we eat?"

The next morning Tahira was visibly tired as she made her way to the dock. Despite her condition she rallied as she saw Jasmina on the dockside. She hugged her friend.

"Please my lady." Jasmina curtsied in front of Tahira and Amir, "Would you find room for a companion on your trip?" Tahira smiled whilst Amir shrugged his shoulders. "There's nothing left here for me now." Amir boarded the ship. Waiting until he was out of earshot, Jasmina continued, "Besides, you might need my help, in the not too distant future. Have you told him yet?"

Tahira smiled, "No, he's been so wrapped up in his work," she paused for moment, "I'm not sure I want to add to his stress levels yet, can we keep this to ourselves for now?"

They departed soon after and headed due north. This was no ordinary sailing ship however as the oarsmen below decks were slaves. They headed out of the harbour to the rhythmical sound of a drumbeat and the occasional crack of a whip. As the wind picked up they stopped rowing and unfurled their sails.

Looking back towards the Persean coastline Tahira thought she could see a large number of ships at anchor just north of Susa. Sadiri advised that they were the remnants of their long abandoned navy. The old ship's timbers were being salvaged and used to construct new housing for the poor.

• • • •

The journey had the outward appearance of being uneventful. With long periods spent in conversation whilst staring out across a vast lake. They were becalmed so the quietness of the day was regularly punctuated with the sound of a drum and a call to row.

The truth was somewhat different. For some time Tahira's dreams had been guiding her in controlling the weather. Since hearing about the drought in Persea she had wondered about whether you could move the rain from one place to another. If she could move particles of dust and sand then could she move the particles in the air?

TAHIRA THE ELEMENTAL

"It's not as easy. The air flows' where it wants and the particles follow. So you have to change the particle itself and then guide it to where you want it to go and the further you move it the more energy is needed."

Tahira had tried experimenting whilst in Queen Makida's palace with varying degrees of success. From a quick gust of wind to blow flies away from food through to moving the threatening rain clouds away on the day of Jasmina's mum's funeral. She still found it exhausting but her recovery times were reducing. She put her developing skills to good use creating small winds to fill the ships sail to lessen the burden on the slaves.

During the day Jasmina's company proved to be invaluable to Tahira as Amir would spend several hours every day with Sadiri discussing plans and options. There was a level of secrecy that Tahira did not appreciate and when she did try to raise it with Amir he quickly dismissed her concerns and changed the subject.

It was sunrise on the fifth day when the call went out that they were approaching the great Mycenean port city of Zakros. The city was no bigger than Susa but there were over 20 ships in the port. Some were trading vessels but others were clearly war machines. All eyes seemed to be focused on them as they made their way slowly from the dockside up to a central civic meeting place. The palace of King Olenus was strictly for private use.

King Olenus was a large rotund man. His thick beard had long turned from black to grey whilst his head was completely clean shaven. He was by nature a suspicious man but cordially welcomed his guests.

After the introductions Sadiri presented King Olenus with some personal gifts including some jewels only found in Persea, garnets, jade and turquoise. In the interests of promoting trade they offered exotic fruits such as watermelons, pomegranates and peaches. There were bronze flagons containing Persean wine. Tahira noted that they conversed in Celta, the universal language of trade and not in Mycenean as she would have expected, at least according to Amir.

Before discussions continued the women were shown to a room off to one side and out of earshot. They were offered refreshments but gracefully declined.

Jasmina and Tahira had worn their face veils but there was no need here. They had seen a few women and without exception their faces where in full view. They sat quietly with Tahira eyeing the two guards who had been placed at the entrance of the door. Subconsciously she ran her fingertips across her belt confirming the presence of her throwing knives.

After a few hours they were invited to re-join their party as they were leaving. No words were said but Tahira glanced across at Jasmina as they seemed to be moving more hurriedly than before. Tahira tripped slightly, only Jasmina helped.

As they reached the wharf where their ship was docked a loud dissonant sound was heard.

"Quick, run!" Sadiri spat the words out. He waved his arms at the captain of their ship, "Get the slaves ready!" he shouted.

Without challenge the rest of the small party took to their heels as the mournful and low hum of the horn continued. Dockers and other workers stopped what they were doing and stared as four strangers ran along a wooden dock desperate to reach the assumed safety of their ship.

TAHIRA THE ELEMENTAL

As the last of them jumped on board so the first stroke of the oar hit the water. The anchor was still being pulled up as ship began to make its way out of the harbour.

"What is going on?" Tahira screamed at Amir.

His reply was terse, "I don't know." He was looking back the dock. A group of men including King Olenus were waving their arms in their direction shouting Celtic obscenities. "I think we might have upset them!"

He turned his ire towards Sadiri, "The King is still alive you idiot!"

"They must have a taster!" Sadiri was shouting above the sound of the drum. They were the last words he spoke as a Mycenean battle ship rammed the bow of their ship. The metallic head had smashed through the wooden rail sending a wooden splinter three cubits long straight through the chest of the now lifeless Sadiri. The ship's captain rallied his men. He had been quick enough to turn the ship away from the enemy so that the he deflected the worst of the impact. They were still afloat. Their ship was smaller than the Mycenean juggernauts. Another battle ship struck them, once again it was just a glancing blow but the enemy were trying to get some of their men on board. They were lucky that a sudden gust of wind forced the ships apart.

They were barely a half a league away from the harbour. There had been other casualties below decks and they were definitely not up to full speed. They presented themselves as a sitting duck as yet another monstrous warship set its sights on the stricken Persean ship. It was however struggling against an unexpected head wind. Yet another warship appeared on the starboard side.

The clouds blackened overhead. A crack of thunder deafened all and a lightning bolt danced across the sky. The air around them started to move in a circular motion, tighter and tighter it wound itself into a spiral that ran across the surface of the lake. It hit one of the Mycenean battleships on its starboard side ripping its central mast asunder as a colossal coruscation of lightning discharged its violent energy into the main deck of the ship. The hull of the mighty ship snapped in half like a twig.

Still the storm gained in strength. The air was as heavy as lead and then a ball of lightening tore across the sky depositing its fury on another of King Olenus's warships. It left a hole on the portside below the water line. Those sailors that could, jumped into the sea and watched as their once mighty fighting ship sank below the waves.

The third warship had turned away from the conflict but to no avail. The storm engulfed it. It was lifted out of the air as a fireball of unimaginable intensity smashed through the hull of the boat and out the other side. The storm raged, its anger needed to be sated further. It headed towards the harbour devouring any ship in its path.

"Time to rest now my child, we are so proud of you."

The Land of the Ice and Snow

"Time to wake up now, you are healed."

Tahira opened her eyes. She was lying on one of her ship's beds with a large sail cloth above her head like a tent.

"She's awake." She heard Jasmina's voice call out before she was swiftly embraced by her, "Are you OK, I was so worried about you?"

Amir came running into the temporary accommodation, "My love, my love, thank the Gods in heaven that you are OK?" Jasmina had graciously left them alone as Amir leant over and kissed Tahira on the forehead. "Look we have salvaged some tea, please drink this, it will make you feel better."

Tahira reached out her hand to hold Amir's. "How are you? Are there many casualties?"

"I'm good now, thanks to you, Sadiri didn't make it, I'm sure Queen Makida will be devastated at his loss." The sarcasm in his voice was obvious, "We lost over half the crew and most of the slaves but, we would all have perished if it wasn't for your 'magic'. So, how long have you been able to control the weather?"

Tahira sat up but was still weary, "I'm not sure I want to talk about it at the moment, so what happened and where are we?"

She moved outside the makeshift tent still holding Amir's hand. She shielded the sun from her eyes, as a shaft of light bounced of the amulet hanging around her neck. Letting go of her hand, Amir held her necklace. "Another quarter has turned blue. Is this the source of your power?"

Tahira gently removed his hand. "Not now Amir, please, just tell me what happened?"

"Well you started waving your arms about and then there was a storm and flashes of lightning and then."

"No, not about me, what happened with King Olenus? Why were we running away, also Sadiri said something about a 'taster'."

"I don't know my love, honestly. I don't know what that horrible little man had done. After our meeting had finished he advised me that we should leave straight away as he had news to give to Makida. When we heard the city's alarm sound we simply panicked, and then you took over and saved us." He laughed, "I doubt the Mycenean will be waging war any time soon." He then paused thoughtfully. "So come on Tahira, how do you do it? You can tell me!"

"Look Amir, maybe it was just a freak storm and we got very lucky OK?"

Tahira turned to walk towards the lake shore before Amir grabbed her arm forcibly, "You will tell me Tahira!" He hissed.

Tahira easily wrestled her arm away from his grip. She knew that the remaining survivors had all turned their gaze towards the couple. She did not want to make a scene so she leant forwards and whispered, "Just because I love you doesn't give you any rights over what I do or say, and, if you love me then you would know that. For now, I will keep my little 'secrets' just as you are keeping yours, my Lord Amir."

She moved away in the direction of the ship's captain whilst Amir turned briskly away and sulked off towards the small wooded area beyond the last of the sand dunes.

TAHIRA THE ELEMENTAL

The ship's captain was nervous. He wasn't entirely convinced that the lady standing in front of him had called the Gods of Thunder to their aid but, he reasoned that it was probably best not to argue that point too much. He cautiously answered all Tahira's questions. "After the storm clouds rolled away we were becalmed and drifted eastwards." He went on to explain how their sails were ripped and beyond quick repair, although they were useful as temporary shelters. They had also sustained quite a lot of damage below decks losing several slaves and oars. Other people sustained injuries and couldn't do anything useful so it was several hours before they could get moving again having cleared and fixed as much of the damage as they could. As night fell they began limping along as best they could but it was only at sunrise that they realised that the rudder had sustained quite a bit of damage below the waterline. He therefore suggested they aim for dry land and that was yesterday morning. "Since then we've been scouring the area looking for more raw materials to finalise the repairs and get back to Susa. We believe that we have landed in Bysyria so we should be relatively safe. However, the surviving slaves ran off last night under the cover of darkness, so, that just leaves me and my men to do the work, and there are only seven of us. So with a lack of materials and men it might be a while before we leave here."

"Why not change the rigging and make the sails smaller. You might not move quickly but you will at least catch some sail?" She looked to turn away but thought of something else, "Also, I'm no expert but have you got any oars left?" The man nodded, "Could you not cut the blades off one or two and somehow strap them onto what is left of the rudder."

The captain had the good sense not to readily dismiss this idea. It took a few moments before his brain engaged and his eyes widened in excitement, "Yes my lady," he was hesitant, the cogs in his mind were slowly getting in to gear, "yes, that might work, well not exactly but, I think we can fashion something." He left Tahira standing there as he walked off towards his men. They were quickly engaged in demonstrative discussions.

Jasmina cuddled into Tahira's arm. "You really are a bit of a marvel, my lady!" She smiled and curtsied. "Come on, they caught some fish yesterday and I bet you are hungry."

Amir arrived back at the camp about an hour or so later. He brought with him an armful of wood for the fire. He was incredibly apologetic and Tahira readily forgave him. It had been a traumatic experience for them all.

Amir woke the next day to find that Tahira was not in his bed. He found her outside of their makeshift shelter staring intently into a newly lit fire. If she had noticed him she didn't show it, he sat down next to her.

"I have to go and find Elita, something's not right!" Tahira's voice was filled with quiet determination. She didn't feel the need to add that her inner voice had told her to go.

"OK." Amir hesitated, "I'll come with you of course, I'll write Queen Makida a letter. Our captain can personally deliver it to her on my behalf."

"Thank you my love but, there is no need, I really appreciate you offering but I know how important your work for your Queen is, I will be fine, you know I can handle myself."

"Of that my love there is no doubt. But..."

Tahira placed a finger on his lips to quell his voice. She leaned across and kissed them softly, "Please, go to your Queen and build that hospital, I will see you at the start of the dry season in Atlassia."

"But that is six months away!" Amir tried to protest but had to accept, albeit reluctantly, that Tahira was not going to change her mind. He was however happy to go back to his Queen. Given that Sadiri was no more, and armed with the latest news about his beloved Tahira, he felt that Makida would reward him well. King Olenus was in no position to make war with Bysyria or anyone else for that matter. Word would soon get round that the mighty empire of Persea could call upon the Gods themselves to smite their enemies. Oh yes, Queen Makida would reward him handsomely, oh and he might get to build that hospital after all.

They sat in silence for a little while until the rest of the camp came to life. Amir went off to discuss the state of the ship's repairs with the captain whilst Tahira quietly made her preparations to leave camp alone.

"So where do you think you are going, my lady?" Jasmina stood at the entrance to the tent used by Amir and Tahira. Her folded arms indicated that she was in no mood to play games.

Tahira smiled, which broadened into a grin as Jasmina swivelled to show Tahira her back on which a fully loaded travelling sack had been strapped. "We," Tahira said pointedly, "are heading north to the land of the ice and snow, there is someone I would like you to meet, I think you will like her, her name is Elita."

Amir arrived back breathless. "We will be leaving shortly. We just need this sail cloth." He pointed to the tent covering. He looked at Jasmina and smiled, "I see your role of companion is safe! Do me a favour please and look after her for me. She has a nasty habit of getting into trouble."

The two women smiled and waved as the remaining survivors of the Persean peoples' ill-fated diplomatic trip to the city of Zakros slowly traversed the calm waters of Lake Mediati. The tiny sails were at odds to the huge bulk of the ship. The damage the vessel had suffered was patched up but still clearly visible. There were only four oars in the water as well.

Tahira imagined that it would take them over a week to complete their journey even with a fair wind. She imagined what a fair wind would look like and how the small sails would billow in that breeze. The ship began to move a little faster through the water. Tahira and Jasmina turned and began their journey north.

They walked for the rest of the day before seeking shelter under a nearby copse of small deciduous trees. As night fell Tahira was reminded about her travelling days with Matai and happily shared the stories with her new travelling companion. Jasmina sat fascinated and kept firing questions at Tahira.

"I would love to meet Matai and Elita. Is Elita a pirate?"

"So many questions my dear Jasmina and I will have plenty of time to answer them but, we need to rest, oh and you can close your mouth, it's not very lady like!" Tahira smiled.

They hadn't walked far in the morning before they saw a small farmhouse. From a place of safety they watched as the farmer and his family went about their daily activities. Tahira pointed to a couple of horses that were being prepared to be attached to a yoke of some description.

TAHIRA THE ELEMENTAL

They inched closer. Tahira imagined a small fire in a nearby animal shelter. She imagined how the small family group would panic and try to put the flame out.

"Now, follow me, keep low." Tahira whispered and Jasmina followed. They quickly made their way past the farmhouse itself and into the small holding pen with the horses. Jasmina quietened the horses and led them out and into a nearby wood. Tahira quickly followed holding a couple of small leather saddles. They moved silently away.

Tahira imagined the look on the faces of the farmer's face when the fire in his animal shelter suddenly went out. She also imagined the look on his face when he realised that his two prized mares had bolted in the commotion. She also imagined the happy face of the farmer's wife when she finds four gold coins on her table, twice the value of the lost horses.

"Four gold coins!" Jasmina was surprised.

"Oh they were a 'gift' from Captain Felix, remember him from the stories I told you last night? Well he left them, and more, to me in his last will and testament." Tahira smiled, "He doesn't need them anymore."

Jasmina recalled the stories that Tahira had told her the previous evening as she had drifted off to sleep. Captain Felix had got his just desserts as far as she was concerned. "Based on what you were saying last night, do you think we should dress as men? Would it be safer?"

Tahira shook her head, such was her new found confidence, "I think we'll be alright." She took out her throwing knives for Jasmina to see, "It won't hurt though for you to gain some new skills along the way. I think it might also be useful to learn my language, it is the language of trade after all."

Jasmina was not as adept as her teacher however she was nonetheless a quick learner.

They saw very few people as they headed north. It took them a couple of days to reach the northern territorial border of the Bysyrian people. There was a river that separated them from the lands of the Mycenea. The river, taking glacial water runoff from the faraway mountains in the east, acted as the main source of water for Lake Mediati.

As they approached they could see small forts on either side of the river. Each was of a similar design with a wooden tower in one corner. It gave them a good vantage point overlooking that stretch of the river. The guards stationed in these turrets paid them little attention as they followed the meandering river upstream, searching for a place to cross.

Eventually they arrived at a heavily fortified bridge crossing with a small camp and village. They watched as merchants paid a toll to official looking individuals on both sides. They joined the small queue.

The Bysyrian toll collector grunted some words at them both. Neither spoke the language but it was clear he wanted to check their bags. Tahira offered him a silver coin which he quickly put in his pocket and waved them on without checking further.

Another silver coin went to the Mycenean border control. Tahira could understand his language well enough but pretended not too. After much arm waving he got bored and allowed them through without further challenge. As it was getting late Tahira suggested that they treat themselves and stay in the village inn.

Yet another silver coin got them a bed for the night plus a meal. Their horses were led to the stables at the back of the inn. They found their Mycenean host to be very friendly and accommodating. After being shown to their room they returned to the bar area for their food.

No one paid them much attention. There was much talk about the recent events in the city of Zakros. Some Persean officials had tried to poison the King but when they tried to capture them a massive storm blew up from nowhere and they lost several ships. The Gods were clearly displeased with them. Someone else said that war between them was inevitable.

A rather drunk young man then noticed Jasmina in the corner. Although her friend was not Persean she clearly was. He approached them both, "What do you think about that then my Persean beauty?" He slurred his words and sat next to Jasmina, uncomfortably close. Jasmina didn't speak the Mycenean language but knew whatever he was saying wouldn't be complimentary. Tahira moved quickly to sit next to their unwanted visitor creating a human sandwich with the drunken man assuming the role of the filling. His friends at the bar watched, laughing before turning back to the barman for more drinks. At that precise moment Tahira took out a throwing knife and using the pommel of it she jabbed it into the man's temple. He slumped into Tahira's shoulder unconscious. She moved back across the table to finish her meal carefully laying the man out along the bench. He was snoring blissfully by the time they went to their room. The other patrons found the whole incident amusing.

Feeling refreshed they left early the following morning. It was the first morning in a while that Tahira hadn't felt a bit of nausea.

"So how many lunar cycles have you got left?" Jasmina was pointing to the Tahira's abdomen.

Tahira smiled, "Well it should be another seven but, it seems to be advancing a lot quicker than expected, I was hoping to help Elita before returning to Atlassia to give birth, hopefully with Amir at my side." Her voice trailed off. It was the first time since waving his ship goodbye that she had thought of the father of her child.

"Well I helped deliver two of my cousin's babies so I can help, if needed. Anyway how long will it take to meet up with Elita?"

Tahira appreciated the change of subject, "Well I don't really know. We are to keep heading north by northwest until we reach the sea. We then hug the coastline heading west for several days at least. But I think it will take us two or three lunar cycles just to get to the sea."

"Am I allowed to know how you know all this also, why does Elita need your help? From what you have told me she is more than capable of looking after herself."

"I'm not sure that you would believe me."

"Go on try me. After all, we do have little bit of time on our hands."

Tahira smiled, she enjoyed Jasmina's company as much as she had enjoyed Matai's at the start of the year. "I hear voices, in my head," Jasmina looked alarmed, "No not like that, when I was a little girl I had an imaginary friend, someone to talk to, someone to tell me things and help me," She laughed, "I once told my father and I remember him smiling at me, he had such a lovely smile, even when he died he was smiling, anyway, he told me that it was my mother looking out for me, her name is Siria, she died when I was born, "

"Good god girl, you haven't had the best of luck have you?"

"Yes well, that's in the past, I can't change it now, so, my imaginary friend still talks to me, mainly in my dreams now, and she told me that I need to go to Elita's place, so that's why."

"What about your special abilities? Where do they come from?"

"Ah that I don't know. My father always said I was special because my mother was special." Tahira hadn't meant to acknowledge her gifts but she trusted Jasmina, "However I don't see my abilities as being special. You have to remember that my so called 'gift' has killed many scores, if not hundreds of men. It does not rest easy on my mind and the worst thing is that part of me thinks that I am not yet finished." She paused but only briefly, "Anyway." Tahira needed to change the subject, "So who came up with the idea about your dead lover Cyrus? Was it your mother or you?"

Jasmina looked shocked, "What?" She stammered, "What are you on about, my lady?"

Tahira tilted her head and raised her eyebrows. She noted a level of discomfort in her friend and decided not to push it further, "Come on," she said, "let's give these horses a bit of exercise shall we?"

The two horses galloped as their riders kept their heads low. All four began to tire after a twenty minute burst of energy. They slowed to a steady walking pace as their adrenalin rush subsided.

"My mother had a mistrust of men, and as I found out fairly recently it was perfectly justified." Jasmina's voice was calm, "After my father died we had nothing, there were days when we didn't eat, the only work she could get involved selling her body, even King Tudiya took an interest, but as she got older she got less and less work. When I became of age some of her acquaintances began to take an interest in me which alarmed my mother. She pleaded with King Tudiya for help and he gave me the job in the palace kitchens."

"Your mother was an amazing woman."

Jasmina nodded, "Thank you, she was. Anyway working in the kitchens has been a real eye opener for me, particularly regarding the older men, they think they can touch me whenever they want, several times when I have fought back they have threatened me, one even tried to have me when I went to the pantry, luckily for me one of the cooks came in and told him where to go, we haven't seen him since, that's when my mother suggested the Cyrus story. We Persean's revere and fear our military in equal measure. So being promised to a soldier meant that I was pretty much left alone. If someone attacked me Cyrus would come home and kill them, justice would be served."

"I clearly have a lot to learn about Persean society" She paused briefly, "But tell me, when did you discover that you preferred the company of women?"

Once more Jasmina looked shocked, she had never told anyone about her feelings or her desires, and yet, "I see my lady has greater skills then I bargained for."

"Let's just put it down to intuition."

TAHIRA THE ELEMENTAL

"Mm, " Jasmina remained unconvinced, "to answer your question, my lady, I am not sure that I have accepted it but what I can tell you is that I have not yet met a man who I have wanted to be intimate with," She paused as she grabbed her horses reins, "come on!" Jasmina pressed the heels of her foot into her horses flank and urged her forward into a gallop.

Tahira accepted that this was the end of that particular conversation and followed her companion.

• • • •

As they journeyed north Jasmina continued with her studies. She struggled with the knives and sword but was a complete natural when it came to her mastery of the bow. Even when riding at full tilt she could hit her targets within a range of sixty paces, forcing the competitive Tahira to keep improving herself.

Jasmina could not compete with Tahira when it came to language. But Tahira was a patient teacher and slowly but surely over the course of their next month's travels Jasmina became comfortable in speaking the Celtic language of trade.

They came to a ridge with the now familiar Mycenean towers denoting the end of King Olenus's reach. Looking both left and right they could make out the wooden forts dispersed along the escarpment. In the twilight they could see flames acting as beacons stretching out as far as the eye could see. It was clear to Tahira that these redoubts had been built and manned for defensive purposes and not trade.

Selecting a suitable copse they made camp for the night. They didn't bother with a cooked meal to avoid creating a visible flame. Their foraged foods provided little in the way of nourishment but it was enough to quell their appetite.

At first light they made their way to the ridge. From their vantage point they could see a vast wetland before them. There was no obvious safe passage through the quagmire.

They heard the tell-tale rumble of horses galloping across the ground and they were heading in their direction.

"I've counted eight of them." Tahira's voice was calm as she dismounted. She motioned for Jasmina to do the same. Jasmina was more nervous. Over the course of the last month's travel they had barely met anyone, especially people in a hurry.

"Oh!" The lead cavalryman was disappointed. "What are you two women doing here, shouldn't you be back home tending to your husbands and children?" He leant forward in his saddle as he sneered.

Tahira bristled, "We are but simple women searching for some lost sheep, we think they may have entered the wetlands. We are looking for a safe passage down this ridge."

He looked closely at them, "I would venture to suggest that with you being a Celt and," he pointed a finger in Jasmina's direction, "she a Persean that it is not just your sheep that are lost." He sat back upright in his saddle, "However today is your lucky day, we don't have the time to teach you some manners. The Agathyrians are attacking us again and I would suggest you abandon your current folly, there is no passage through that hell scape down there, your sheep will be dead, and so will you be if, you don't get back to your village and warn your people."

With a quick flick of his wrist, his horse turned and sped off heading east towards the ice topped mountains in the distance. One rider held himself back. He was a young man, he

TAHIRA THE ELEMENTAL

didn't look at Tahira, his eye was turned by Jasmina's beauty. "If you head about five hundred paces westward you will come to some spiky gorse bushes. There is a narrow gap, just wide enough for you to lead your horse through, my father told me about an old trackway he used when hunting." Jasmina smiled and beckoned the young man to come closer. As he bowed down she reached up on her tiptoes and kissed him on the cheek. He blushed and rode off to catch up with the others.

"What? Are we not grateful for his help?" said Jasmina as she faced Tahira.

They could see the gorse bushes and so led their horses in that direction. The trackway was not obvious but with Tahira taking the lead they carefully made their way to the bottom of the bluff. Their hearts sank however, when they realised that the four foot high water reeds presented a formidable obstacle.

Remounting their steeds they spent a good thirty minutes or so walking up and down the mud bank probing for a safe way into the marsh. Despite their skills as accomplished horse women, they had to work hard to prevent their mares from becoming skittish and flighty.

They pursued a couple of dead ends before finally finding a thin strip of land that hadn't been fully covered by the water. Once more Tahira took the lead as they inched slowly forward. She paused frequently to check that they were not going round in circles. The meandering nature of the trackway was disorientating.

Tahira found her mind wandering off, lost in a daydream. She wondered what it would be like if this trackway was just a little bit higher above the water. With a subtle wave of her hand she began to bring other nearby soil particles and added them to the path she was on. She felt the ground beneath her rise forcing the water reeds apart ever so slightly. The change was barely noticeable but it was enough.

Watching from behind Jasmina was surprised to see that just as they approached the thickest part of the wetland so their path ahead became easier to follow. The air was still, even the birdsong had fallen silent bewitched as she was herself.

It was mid-afternoon by the time they made it through the wetland to be greeted by another cliff edge. This was not as steep as on the Mycenean side of the basin but nonetheless unsure of finding an easy pathway they decided to make an early camp and give themselves as much daylight as possible to tackle the ascent. Tahira's baby kicked inside her as she dismounted.

The morning greeted them with a bright but chilly sunrise. The light danced between the cliffs and crevices creating ever changing shadows, each hinting at a pathway with which to ascend the bluff. They had a couple of false starts before finding their way up the escarpment. What lay ahead of them was a large and relatively dense forest. Although tricky to traverse it did provide them with plenty of cover as they meandered through this unforgiving and unknown land.

Over the course of the next couple of weeks as they continued on their journey northwards they saw very few people. Mainly subsistence farmers working the few open patches of cleared woodland. Of those people they observed they found it curious that they saw no young men. They had much to learn about Agathyrian society.

The further north they headed the more dispersed the forest became. At the same time they began to see more and more of the people of Agathyria. They reached a large area of open land which had several trackways heading in varied directions.

They decided to take cover in a nearby copse. They spent a few hours in the morning watching and waiting. They needed to get across this land but they would be exposed with little chance to seek cover or shelter if needed. They observed a small collection of carts laden with various goods heading roughly in their required direction. It mainly consisted of a ragtag bunch of people walking alongside the carts, although some rode on the backs of small ponies.

Gathering their resolve they joined the back of this train. They pulled their coat collars up and pulled their hats down to try and hide their faces as much as possible. They trudged along the pathway as slowly and desperately as their fellow travellers.

Nobody paid them any attention as they moved across the plain. Occasionally young men dressed in black uniforms, and on horseback, would come streaking past them. Tahira noted that the bald headed, middle aged man sitting on the lead cart would bow his head and offer a salute to these men. He was clearly the leader of these merchants.

Progress was slow throughout the afternoon. Lost in their thoughts they came to a shuddering stop to avoid careering into the stationary cart in front of them. They could see a small commotion ahead of them. The leader was gesticulating to a thickset, bearded man clearly issuing orders of some description. Tahira dismounted and handed her reins to a concerned Jasmina.

"Stay here, I just want to have a quick look." She whispered out of earshot of the rest of the caravan.

She moved quietly and quickly towards the front of the train. No one noticed, they were clearly frightened by what was unfolding in front of them. The large bearded man dismounted and began to examine the contents of the cart. He turned to one of the five men mounted on black stallions. In a language unfamiliar to Tahira they had a brief heated exchange. A woman riding a small pony alongside the main cart shouted back at the two men.

The bearded man stopped in his tracks and walked threateningly over to the young woman. In a swift, decisive movement he plucked her from her mount and threw her to the ground. Turning to the leader of the merchants he said something that caused him to shake with visible rage. Before he could remonstrate further a sword was thrust against his neck. The bearded man's main accomplice nodded at the leader before slowly withdrawing his sword.

The bearded man picked the young woman up by her hair. Forcing her head back he leant in to kiss her. She spat in his face causing the rest of the assailants to laugh. With a mocking grin he wiped the spit from his face before punching that pretty face to the ground.

His next punch was stopped. He watched the blood trickle from his victim's young face before slowly turning to see who had grabbed his arm.

He looked into Tahira's face. A face as young as the one he had just beaten to the ground. For a moment he just stared as Tahira released his arm.

"Well, well, well, what have we here? A Celt if I'm not mistaken?" His gruff voice complimented his robust features. His immediate change to converse in Tahira's native language almost caught her off guard. A gentle murmur spread throughout the rest of the travelling caravan.

"In that sense you have the advantage of me sir." Tahira's voice was full of sarcasm. She bowed her head keeping her eyes firmly on her adversary.

"You are a long way from home, my lady, and the treaty between your people and mine prevents you from interfering with our internal affairs, so as a captain of the Agathyrian army I would kindly ask you to step away and honour your country's agreement."

"And if I don't?" Tahira didn't need to look. She knew that the sword that was previously pressed against the neck of the old man was now pointing in her direction.

The captain reached down and punched the kneeling woman back to the ground. Tahira sighed, "Honour, and what do you know about honour?"

She stepped back a couple of paces but this was no retreat. She needed the room to free her arms. Silently and sequentially each of the men who remained on horseback slumped forward on to their horse's neck. If they had remained alive they would have appreciated the precision with which each of the throwing knives had killed them. Tahira smiled to herself, the captain hadn't even noticed. However the man with the sword did and he moved threateningly forward raising his sword arm. He was too slow, hampered further by the sudden loss of movement to his legs. Tahira had swiftly and deftly somersaulted herself to stand behind her attacker. She removed her dagger from his lower spine before cutting the man's throat as the final cry of anguish left his body.

The captain had become all too aware that things had not gone the way he had planned it. What was to be a routine bit of extortion, followed by a bit of fun with a young woman, had been compromised by a Celt and a female one at that. He had little time left for any more thoughts. His life force was ebbing away. He knew something sharp and metallic had been plunged into his heart. He waited for the dark to engulf him and the oblivion that followed.

Tahira heard a sharp whistle and watched in admiration as various members of her travelling companions went to work. The six militia men were placed in different carts and covered by sack cloth as were each of the horse's saddles. The stallions themselves were attached to the last of the carts. Jasmina had moved forward. She cleaned the bloodied face of the young woman and got her back onto her horse.

Within minutes they were once more moving forwards as if nothing had happened. The group's leader indicated to Tahira to ride alongside him.

"Thank you and your friend, my name is Namud." His youthful voice was in marked contrast to his obvious age. He was not comfortable speaking Tahira's language and it was heavily accented but she was grateful nonetheless.

Tahira in turn introduced herself and Jasmina. She had no reason to distrust him.

They rode on in relative silence for another league or so. As the last of the sunlight sank in the western sky the old man pointed towards the northern horizon, "We make camp now." Namud raised his hand and released another high pitched whistle. He led the caravan a few hundred paces off the trackway. Everyone else knew what their responsibilities were.

Fires were lit, animals were fed and watered and food was prepared.

Tahira and Jasmina were invited to stay with them which they gratefully accepted. The conversation was stilted and involved the use of a lot of hand gestures. It was however pleasant, although burying the six dead assailants caused them some internal reflection.

Whilst the rest of the troupe pitched their tents Tahira and Jasmina snuggled up as near to the fire as they possibly could. The embers providing just enough warmth to keep out the night chill.

The morning decampment was organised and efficient. These travelling merchants were old hands at the game. Namud had explained as best he could that they were going to deliver their goods to the market that supplied food and chattels to the large training fort a few miles ahead of them. They would then be heading north again after the day's trading. Tahira and Jasmina would be welcome to travel with them. It was an invite which they readily accepted.

As Namud and his company set up their market stalls Tahira and Jasmina took the opportunity to melt away into the crowds milling around the fort and its associated collection of buildings known locally as Old Town.

They found a local seamstress who was selling hooded capes made from fine sheep's wool. They agreed that they would be perfect to keep out the chill as they ventured further north. A silver coin was enough to secure one each of the dark grey cloaks which they put on immediately.

Their faces where now better hidden as they continued their aimless wanderings. They were grateful for this when they spotted some men moving through the market. They were dressed in black, similar to the outfit the captain and his men had been wearing the day before. There were three of them aggressively pushing people out of their way. Occasionally stall holders would offer them some of their goods, others gave coins. If anyone dissented they were beaten with a stick.

"They are our beloved Militia Guards, come with me, you don't need to make a scene, I have a lovely pot of pine tea on the go, come on, I'm not going to hurt you." A middle aged woman had gently placed her hand on Tahira's arm. She had carefully avoided the throwing knife it held and had purposefully placed herself between Tahira and the Militia Guards thus preventing her from using it whilst also shielding it from any onlookers.

Tahira shook off the old woman's hand and hid her arm under the cape although her fingers remained caressing the blade.

"My name is Morgana, come, I might be able to answer some of your questions."

Tahira nodded reluctantly and with a shrug of her shoulders followed Morgana's lead. A silent Jasmina stepped in line alongside Tahira who kept her hand on the haft of her dagger. They went through a few small alleyways until they reach a wooden hovel. Morgana beckoned them inside.

Tahira had no sense of foreboding so entered willingly and was immediately surprised as to the size and cleanliness of the inside of the building. It was the complete opposite to the outside. They were offered a couple of chairs to sit in next to a fire enclosed in a metal box with air vents in it. They were presented with a hot and freshly brewed pine tea for which Tahira was especially grateful.

TAHIRA THE ELEMENTAL

"So you must be Tahira and you are her companion, Jasmina, oh and please forgive my accent, I am a little rusty in speaking Celtic, it's been more years than I care to remember since I left my childhood home." Morgana was intently looking into Tahira's eyes as if seeking something, "I must admit I was expecting you both to be a bit older."

Jasmina looked shocked. If Tahira shared that feeling she didn't show it. "Are you claiming to be an Oracle, Morgana?" Tahira interrupted without raising her voice. She reached out to her inner voice but received no reply.

Morgana laughed, "An Oracle? Oh no! Not me my lady." She paused briefly, "I prefer the term, soothsayer." She raised her hands and voice dramatically.

"You're a fortune teller, oh how exciting!" Tahira's voice dripped with sarcasm as she smiled at Jasmina. "I wouldn't have thought that we would be your average customer, Morgana."

A slightly deflated Morgana replied, "Apparently not, my skills are however unparalleled. How else would I have known you were coming and, your names, don't forget that?"

"Ok, Mistress Soothsayer, what is it that you want."

Morgana sighed, "Look I understand your lack of faith in what I am telling you and trust me there are times when I struggle with the idea myself." She laughed, "However much to my own personal annoyance and some of my clients, I am really good at this and maybe the best there is. Now do drink your tea my dear."

Tahira instinctively did as she had been requested. It had been many weeks since she had last tasted its sweet refreshment, "At the risk of repeating myself. What do you want from us?"

"Me? Oh nothing. Well, that's not strictly true I suppose." Morgana placed her hands carefully on the table, "Look, despite your misgivings, as I mentioned previously I am very good at this. However my latest visions only tell me so much and I can't see beyond a certain point, they become blurred and confused. This has never happened to me before." She sipped her tea, she looked at the blank expressions on the faces of her guests before continuing, "Let me explain, I have had the skill of foresight for all my life, my parents would bring people to me and I would tell them their future, when they should plant their crops, whether they would have a boy or a girl etc. Simply touching their temple would be enough for me to see what was going to happen to them in response to a specific question. In the beginning I didn't always get it right but over the years my skills developed as did the accuracy of my visions. However these visions have always been for the benefit of someone else but my latest vision is for me. It's my future that I see but you, a baby girl and a mother figure play a part and that's the bit I can't see."

She stopped talking and leant back in her chair. Tahira's unborn child kicked at the mention of a baby girl. "If you are as good as you say you are then you will know what I am about to say."

"There is no need and there is also no debate. I am ready and will join you for the next part of your journey to visit Elita's home. Are you finished with your tea?" Morgana stood up and smiled at Tahira whose face could not hide her shock at the words she had just heard, "I will ride on one of the carts, riding horses is bad for my back."

TAHIRA THE ELEMENTAL

"But..." Tahira's words faded away. She and Jasmina followed the flaxen haired woman out of the door and onto the streets of the Old Town.

The market traders were packing up, some had already left. They found Morgana in conversation with Namud. She handed him a small coin purse. He didn't open it but merely moved it up and own in his hand as if weighing the unknown contents. He smiled and offered her a seat on his cart next to him. She reminded him of his long dead wife. Tahira and Jasmina mounted their horses and took their place at the back of the pack of travelling traders. True to Namud's word they headed north and away from Old Town and its fort. As night began to fall they turned off the dirt road and set up camp at the edge of small clump of trees.

Morgana was the centre of attention at the camp that night. She regaled her fellow travellers with tales of places and people that Namud and his companions could only dream about. They hung on her every word. Although unable to completely understand every word Jasmina and Tahira also found themselves swept up in the stories told by this soothsayer.

That night Morgana chose to sleep under the stars in the company of Tahira and Jasmina.

"That was quite a show." Jasmina ventured.

"Why thank you Jasmina, glad you enjoyed it, it is all true by the way, every word of it."

"No one could prove otherwise, could they?" The smile on Tahira's face was as warm as the fire lit glow in her cheeks.

"You are a very old for someone so young my lady Tahira, so what is your story then?"

"Before I tell you anything, I am curious to know about the Agathyrians and how a Celt like yourself ended up here. I didn't even know these people existed until we reached their country."

"Oh that's easy, in common with most humankind the Agathyrian people are driven by greed and power. For them their dogma centres on dominance and they achieve that through war. Tact and diplomacy are an anathema to them. All young men from the age of fourteen upwards are taken off to training camps like the fort we were at yesterday in the Old Town. Everything and everyone else is subservient to the military. They are taught to fight and to take whatever they want from their enemies. Those who are successful become even more powerful. Sometimes however it spills into normal life. They are not supposed to steal from their fellow countrymen but the authorities tend to turn a blind eye. Some of them will form small militia groups like you saw earlier today. They supposedly offer 'protection' to business owners for a small fee but more often than not they simply behave like common thugs."

Tahira interrupted, "It seems to me that all the tribes of this world are on some sort of war footing. Are all men born to hate?" Her words trailed off as she shook her head in disgust.

"They hate through ignorance, their greed makes them blind to understanding and their lust for power is all consuming. It is easier for a man to see the world through a set of blinkers rather than open their eyes to the possibilities offered through tolerance, education and love." Morgana paused, but only briefly, "My visions tell me that man is on a pathway to self-destruction, putting an end to the world as we know it. In this particular instance I hope my visions are wrong, but as I have mentioned previously, they rarely are."

"So why are you here then?" Tahira had calmed down. She was beginning to warm to Morgana.

"Oh that's easy. The Agathyrian people are incredibly superstitious. Their society is all about their war machine. Everything else is merely an enabler, and the biggest facilitator of this is ignorance. These people are the least educated I have ever come across in all my travels. Did you know, for example, that there are no schools? Well, as long as you don't count the military training ones." She paused and took a deep breath of the cold night air, "It's this ignorance that allows the so called leaders to control the masses. And, they use superstitions to help reinforce that control so someone like me can make quite a good living with my scrying skills." She nodded to herself as if waiting for her listeners to agree. She had come to realise that these two were not like her other clients. She shook her head, "However, several lunar cycles ago I started having my end of the world visions. The residents of Old Town began to think that I might have gone a bit crazy and sometimes I have to agree with them." She laughed, "And now it's your turn."

"Well I am but an ex-slave."

As Tahira began Jasmina closed her eyes. She had heard this before. She didn't make it to the end but was awake long enough to hear Morgana interject with questions as well as various excitable noises. Tahira for her part kept the story brief. Her abilities were not for public discussion. Jasmina had caught a glimpse of what she could do but no one else need know.

As Tahira closed her eyes her unborn baby made its presence known. In her dreams she saw the end of the world.

They continued heading north, northwest for the next few days. They saw little in the way of other people. There was the odd small farmstead from whom they were able to buy meat and milk. One of the farmers recognised Namud and the whole caravan of travellers were offered refreshments whilst Namud and his friend spoke at length about trade and of Namud's recent trip to Old Town.

Morgana acted as a translator for Tahira and Jasmina. Before they left Namud's friend advised him to steer clear of the northern coastline. Apparently word has reached the Agathyrian King that the hated Norsemen from Skandia were busy amassing ships and soldiers in readiness to cross the Norse Sea. The king has sent several battalions north to protect their coast from potential invasion.

They could see Namud shaking his head. He was complaining that wherever they went all anyone could talk about was war. He then went on to tell his friend that he was getting too old for all this travelling. It was not that he expected to die from old age, very few people did, but he was letting his acquaintance know that he was planning on going back to his homeland in the mountains with his remaining family and becoming a farmer himself.

After the formalities were over they carried on with their journey. At that evening's camp Namud asked to speak with Tahira and Jasmina. Morgana would translate although of course Tahira had been taking lessons from her inner voice and understood perfectly what everyone was saying but hadn't yet decided to let her companions know.

TAHIRA THE ELEMENTAL

Namud reached into his pocket and pulled out a gold coin. He had managed to sell the five stallions in the Old Town market but as the horse trader knew that they were militia horses he hadn't got as much as he had hoped. Tahira knew that Namud would have gotten more than he was offering her but it was of no consequence, she didn't need the money and she requested Morgana to tell him to keep it as payment for escorting them this far north.

Namud nodded and quickly put the coin back in the lining of his coat. He then advised that in the morning he would take the three of them as far as the mountain pass which leads into Juteria. He and his family would then head east and into the mountains of his homeland. Morgana then engaged in conversation with Namud. Tahira understood what was being debated but decided to let them argue it out as she and Jasmina went and found somewhere warm to spend the night.

"Morgana's not very happy with Namud is she?" Jasmina yawned.

"You are correct. Somehow I think we will be enjoying the company of our friends for a little bit longer yet." Tahira smiled before gazing at the brightest star in the night sky. They both pulled their hooded cloaks about them and drifted off to sleep.

The ever decreasing temperatures indicated that winter was well on its way. This was even more evident as they reached the mountains that protected the north western border of Agathyria at noon the next day.

When the train of carts came to a halt in a small border settlement Morgana walked back to Tahira and Jasmina.

"Namud wants to know if your friends in Juteria have items that he could buy and trade."

"From what my father told me they trade animal skins, dried fish and lamp oil. I also believe that they are master knife makers." Tahira offered.

"Good, that's settled then. We will take you to meet your friend before Namud becomes a farmer."

"Aren't you supposed to give him my answers first, you know, to let him make his decision?"

Morgana smiled, "Let's just say that he has got his eye's set on a bigger prize! I may not be a spring chicken anymore but I know a thing or two about how to keep a man happy!"

The mountain pass took them high up and level with the clouds. The animals struggled to pull the carts towards their destination. Even Namud was forced to walk alongside his beasts of burden to ease their suffering. Fortunately, although the climb was arduous it was short. They quickly got their breath back as they began their descent into Juteria. As the clouds began to break they were greeted with a beautiful vista of lowland valleys broken into a patchwork of fields and small woodlands. Small glacial streams and rivers cut through the land below them like bolts of lightning arcing their way across the sky.

They were surprised to see that there was little more than a trading post to greet them as they entered this luscious land. They readily bought some fresh bread from a market trader who, after trying several different languages, spoke to them in perfect Agathyrian.

The Norsemen Approach

They travelled at a slow and steady pace for several days until they reached the sea. Although wary of strangers the people they met were welcoming and willing to sell whatever produce they had available.

They made camp on a cold crisp night on a beach overlooking the ocean. It was a full moon and the waters were calm. Tahira was aware that she would soon give birth ten or twelve weeks earlier than expected. She was however not fearful for her baby, her inner voice had told her it was perfectly healthy. She trusted that voice although some of her dreams of late were more nightmarish.

Tahira woke with a start. Sunrise was still a couple of hours away. In the moonlight she could make out a figure walking slowly around the camp. It was Morgana. Tahira went to her but Morgana was lost in a trance like state. It was broken when Tahira reached out to her. The physical contact snapped Morgana back to reality. She almost crumpled to the floor and needed Tahira to hold her steady.

The embers of the nearby fire had kept the water hot enough to make a fresh cup of pine tea. Having reached an area of abundant supply, Namud's family of travellers had rapidly added the consumption of pine tea to their daily routine.

"I see your visions." Tahira whispered as she handed Morgana a reviving brew. "I have been having them since we met you in The Old Town."

Morgana was confused, "But you are not a soothsayer, are you?"

Tahira shook her head, "In truth I don't know what I am, as a child I knew I was different, my father was a clever man and he taught me things that other children my age could not understand, I have an inner voice that guides me as well, it also gives me knowledge when I sleep and occasionally it gives me warnings that affect the people I love and I have learned to respond to it as an invisible early warning system." Tahira was aware that she had not told as much as this to anyone before, even Matai did not know.

"Would you like me to look?" Morgana's voice was weak, almost trembling.

Tahira held her hand, "Thank you but the last person who tried ended up as a pile of dust at my feet." She quickly added, "It was not of my making." She paused briefly, "I like you Morgana so I will carry on as is and it will eventually become clear to me."

Morgana rallied a little, "Well the offer stands but I have to say that I am a little weak at the moment. It may be for the best, for both of us."

"So your vision tonight involved me then?"

"How could you know that?" Morgana couldn't deny the truth of it, although she was struggling to interpret it.

"As I said, I have seen some of your visions for myself and there was a look of horror on your face when you came out of your trance to see me holding you so I put two and two together."

"I fear for you Tahira as well as for all mankind. I cannot reconcile my dreams nor your role in those dreams. For the first time in my life I see my gift as a curse!" She paused briefly before rallying, "However before any of that, we need to get you to Elita's and you need to give birth to your daughter."

"So my dear Morgana, how did you know my name, Jasmina's and Elita's?"

"Oh that's the easy bit. I had been following you around the market for a while and heard bits of your conversation. You called each other by your names when you were buying your hooded capes and at one point you mentioned about going to see Elita."

"I see," said Tahira, "Sometimes the ability to listen is the greatest skill any of us can possess."

They laughed and talked some more as they watched the sunrise.

They left later that morning heading east but sticking to the coast. Tahira didn't know where she was going, nor did anyone else. However, no one questioned it, if Tahira wanted to go somewhere they would follow. After a couple of days the coastline guided them north once more. At this point they found and followed a small dirt track road. This pathway ran through several small villages. They were told by a local that the road led to their capital city Kobenharven. This reassured her that they were not too far from their intended destination.

It was nearly a week before they reached the outskirts of the capital city of the Jutes. Although it was cold and the worse of winter was yet to show its hand, this land was not as described in the myths and legends Tahira had been told as a child. The people were not blood thirsty, violent savages. Also their country was not enshrouded in ice and snow. This was a green land populated by farmers and fisher folk.

Namud and his family made camp half a league from the outskirts of the sprawling township. They were on a small hill and could see multiple ships in the natural harbour. Tahira recognised one of those ships. She pointed out Aija to Jasmina.

It was still early afternoon so Tahira and Jasmina decided to head to the dock area.

As they dismounted and tied up their horses Tahira saw Elita. Although she had her back to them it was clear that the imposing figure in front of them was the intrepid mariner they sought. Elita was barking orders to her men as they unloaded their precious cargo of pots all the way from the city of Atlassia. Even from this view her curvaceous figure and short cropped blonde hair cut her out as a female of some importance.

"You might want to close your mouth, it's not very ladylike!" Tahira gently teased Jasmina as they pulled their hoods over their heads and approached the pirate queen.

"Excuse me young lady but could I buy one of those pots please?" Tahira stood behind Elita.

There was a short pause before Elita spoke, "Why of course madam, they are the best quality and come from the great city of Atlassia."

"You always were my favourite pirate you know!" Tahira removed her face covering as did Jasmina.

Elita shrieked, "Tahira. Praise be given to the sky gods!" She turned sharply and embraced her friend before she barked some orders at her crew.

They stepped away from the ship and had a brief catch up. Jasmina was introduced and Tahira noticed a glint in her eyes. When she had first met Lucretus the slave she appeared quiet, even withdrawn. But when she released the shackles and became Elita once more she cut an imposing and attractive figure. A confident young woman with a zest for life and if there was something she didn't know about ships and sailing it wasn't worth knowing.

"So when were you going to tell me you were pregnant?" Elita placed her hand on Tahira's stomach just as the baby kicked.

"Well, I wasn't when I last saw you."

Elita scoffed. "Some friend you are. Another one of your little secrets was it, bet you and Amir had a little laugh about it did you, talking of which where is the soon to be father?"

"Well that's another story, as you know we went to Persea to help them with their drought, well long story short Amir offered to build them a hospital and he is still there now, I will however see him in three lunar cycles back in Atlassia and present him his child, although it might come as a surprise to him as he doesn't know."

Elita was shaking her head, "You are not a normal person Tahira. Do you know that?" She looked across at Jasmina who smiled.

"So tell me Jasmina, how did you end up being friends with this abnormal human being?"

Jasmina was initially reluctant to speak but once she found her voice she regaled Elita with all the events that had happened since she had met Tahira, including how she had defeated the navy of King Olenus.

Tahira tried to interrupt on several occasions but Elita waved her objections away. Elita knew that Tahira would be more reticent and self-deprecating. Clearly the two of them had been through a lot together and any friend of Tahira's was a friend of Elita's.

They spent another hour or so chatting before one of Elita's crew approached her to say that the unloading was complete. They went their separate ways after agreeing to meet again the next day.

That night a storm rolled in from the north. Tahira and Jasmina were grateful to be under cover as the bitter wind buffeted their tent walls. Morgana saw it as a portent of things to come.

By the early morning the storm had passed. Although still cloudy, it was dry by the time Tahira and Jasmina arrived at their planned meeting point. Morgana had insisted that she accompany them. Whilst walking through the city Tahira noted that it was significantly quieter than the previous day. The few people they had seen appeared more sullen, more circumspect. It was as if the clouds in the sky were weighing heavy on the people of Kobenharven.

Morgana didn't wait to be introduced. Elita forced a smile but eventually had to confess that today was not a good day. "News has reached my father over night that the Norsemen from the East are massing their ships, they are planning for war." Her voice was tinged with anger, "We have tales about the last time they made war against us. It cost the lives of thousands of men and for what, we eventually drove them back but the cost was enormous, on both sides. We spread the word that we drank their blood and that we tortured them both slowly and painfully. We spread rumours that we relished putting our enemies to death in ever increasingly horrific and ritualistic ways. We created our own myths and legends as a way to ensure peace between ourselves and our neighbours. It worked for several generations but now, now we have forgotten how to fight whilst they have grown in numbers and in desperation. They are desperate to avenge the deaths of their forefathers and to expand their borders and enslave those who survive the hell that they are about to unleash." Her voice trailed off but what she described matched Morgana visions. "He thinks he can persuade them to change their minds, he has sent word to the Norse king and requested Parlay. He will set sail tonight."

Tahira's baby kicked and kicked hard.

"Will you go with him?" Jasmina's softly spoken voice cut through the silence.

"Sadly my father sees 'ruling' as man's work. I am more capable than my younger brothers but they are next in line, not me. No, I shall wait here like the rest and wait and hope. Besides Aija needs a few repairs so I will busy myself with that and let my crew have some time off." Elita had regained her composure.

"Can I help? I liked to learn a bit more about ships." Jasmina surprised herself before looking over at Tahira who smiled. Elita too glanced across at Tahira, before accepting Jasmina's offer of assistance.

"I think we shall go back to camp and rest up." Morgana had also switched her attention to Tahira but not to seek some sort of approval. She had sensed that Tahira's baby daughter was becoming more and more restless inside her.

It was early evening when Tahira went into labour. Morgana had helped deliver babies before but this was going to be difficult. The rest of Namud's family lacked any real experience but they were good for fetching cloths and warm water. They had some willow bark for Tahira to chew on but it barely took the edge off the pain. At times Tahira was delirious, she called out Amir's name several times desperately wanting to hold him to help her through. Her inner voice tried to be calming and encouraging but the baby presented herself feet first.

As soon as Morgana realised the baby was breeched she got Tahira to change her position. From her experience she knew a breech birth was easier on all fours. Still the baby girl struggled for freedom. Realising that the umbilical cord was wrapped around a leg Morgana worked swiftly to clear it out of the way. With a final excruciating push baby Astra came into the world on the stroke of midnight.

"Welcome to the world baby Astra, as beautiful as her mother. Tahira we love you so much. Now rest."

An excited Elita and Jasmina burst through the tent door to find Tahira sipping her pine tea with her daughter cradled in her arms. Morgana had sent word.

Tahira smiled as she handed her daughter over to Elita, "This is my daughter Astra, Astra say hello to your Aunt Elita and Aunt Jasmina." As if choreographed Astra smiled at each new face she was presented too. Her azure blue eyes sparkled as hearts melted. As Astra yawned Morgana placed her into a fleece line rush basket to sleep, which she readily did.

"Has there been any news of your father?" Tahira was sore and achingly tired but despite her recent somewhat traumatic experience she was still keen to know of any updates regarding the Norsemen and the Juteri.

"No, not yet. If I am honest I do not believe he will succeed. The remaining civic leaders have agreed that should he not return by nightfall then we will muster as many ships as we can and sail to confront them." Elita paused, "In the meantime we must prepare for the worst."

"I have been showing some of the men how to make and fire the flaming arrows, the way you taught me Tahira." Jasmina had remained quiet but there was a steely determination in her voice.

"Good, that will certainly help. What about your town defences? Where are your weak points? They are less likely to attack a well defended harbour but is there somewhere near where they can land and attack the city from the rear?" Tahira had no experience of military planning and yet it made sense to her. More importantly it triggered something in Elita's mind, giving her food for thought.

Tahira noted how close Elita and Jasmina were sitting next to each other, almost touching, "I like your new outfit Jasmina, a pirate queen and a pirate princess." She smiled.

Jasmina blushed ever so slightly.

Tahira reached across and placed her hand on Elita's knee, "It's OK, the world is changing, even if it is incredibly slowly, Aunt Elita. Besides we are all friends here."

Elita raised her eyebrows, "You are a marvel my dear Tahira but, a little misguided, the Jutes and the other peoples of this world are not yet ready for such things. We need to manage expectations."

"Rather than manage, maybe we need to lead, my dear Elita." Tahira knew that if they could avert war this time that change would be required or it would only be a matter of time before the cycle of war repeated.

Elita stood up and hugged her friend, "Come, we have work to do. We need to prepare the people of Kobenharven." Jasmina followed her out of the tent.

Morgana ushered Tahira back into bed, "Whilst Astra is sleeping you may as well get some rest yourself, you will need it!"

Tahira's sleep was disturbed. She dreamt of steep sided valleys rising out of the ocean. She saw icebergs floating in the fjords. These bergs slowly turned into ships before metamorphosing back into large, slow moving blocks of ice the size of a farmhouse. She thought she could hear the screams of lost souls but could see no one. Fog rolled down the valley sides shrouding everything in a haunting mist. It settled across the water. She saw hands reaching up through the vaporous miasma. Clawing and grasping. She held out her hand but they were only shadows, wispy and ethereal. Still she heard the cries of the lost and abandoned. Then there was silence, abrupt and deafening. In her mind she saw a sea fog roll across the land before the haar quickly dissipated revealing a landscape bereft of life. The sea was frozen and the land was covered in snow. She looked heavenward to see one star shining brightly in the night sky. Was it a beacon of hope, a celestial guide to a better future? Tahira woke from her restless slumber with an unanswered question etched into her heart.

Astra was being entertained by Morgana. It only served to increase the sense of foreboding that Tahira felt. She longed for Amir to be at her side.

As the last vestiges of daylight spread their tentacles across the land of the Jutes, Namud and his family of travelling merchants looked out towards the eastern skyline. Tahira,

TAHIRA THE ELEMENTAL

clutching Astra to her chest, joined them to watch the 13 ships leave the safety of Kobenharven harbour. Silently and collectively they sent a prayer to their own gods for the safe return of all hands. Jasmina was not ready for the fight to come but even though it had only been a few days she knew in her heart that she would rather die with Elita than live without her.

"I should have gone with them Morgana, they might need me." The concern in Tahira's voice was clear to anyone within earshot.

"Aye they might but, Astra definitely needs you." She paused briefly before smiling, "I mean look at me. I am well past being a wet nurse."

It lifted Tahira's spirits a little, "When did your visions stop?"

Morgana was caught off guard and tried to rubbish the idea but realising the truth she shook her head as she acceded, "The second Astra was born, I felt different, it had been clear to me for several months that I needed to be with you, to help you with her birth, once my job was done I felt like an enormous weight had been lifted off my shoulders." She wept. Tahira comforted her before Morgana continued, "Having visions, seeing into the future, it's all I have ever known. Yes there have been times I wished for it to be different but to suddenly lose it." She took a deep breath, "It's weird. I feel a sense of grief for the loss. I can't describe it in any other way but, it's also liberating. It's like someone has removed a set of blinkers from my eyes, I am seeing the world in a new and clear light. The moment I looked into your daughter's eyes my life changed forever." Right on queue Astra squirmed in her mother's arms to face Morgana, she opened her eyes and smiled. "You see, you see what I mean. No one day old baby should be able to do what she does. It's as if she understands."

"It is I who should be grateful to you, without you I don't know that I, we, could have made it. You know I never knew my mother, she died in childbirth and..." Tahira didn't finish her sentence, she didn't need to. A single tear fell from her eye as she headed back into the tent and out of the cold. Strangely she felt more alone than ever before, she held Astra tight to her breast.

For the first time in many years Morgana slept well, free from visions. Tahira was not so fortunate. Once more she dreamt of frozen seas and wondered how such a vast ever moving ocean could cease its motion. Once more she saw hands reach out to her but this time they were trapped in the ice. She could see hundreds of wide eyed, open mouthed faces trapped in the ice, their screams of despair forever silenced.

The next day was spent resting. Tahira stayed in Namud's camp although some members ventured into the town. People were doing their best to maintain a sense of normality. The community worked on defences as best they could. But with each passing hour, without sight of the ships, the mood darkened. As the evening approached those who had the means began to leave the town. They packed what they could into carts and left in droves. The younger members of Namud's troupe became even more restless as each cart passed along the road next to their camp. The look of fear on the faces of the town's people was clear for all to see. They didn't know where they were going they only knew that they needed to be as far away from Kobenharven as possible. Some of the more emboldened 'remainers' jeered and whistled as the self-imposed refugees trudged along the pathway. A society divided without a word being spoken.

It was yet another bitterly cold night. Tahira woke an hour before sunrise but there was no going back to sleep. She fed Astra before placing her in a papoose around her chest. Leaving their tent they set out on their walk to the headland south of the city. From there she knew she would get the first glimpse of the returning ships, or as she feared, what was left of them. She had barely closed the flap on her tent when Morgana joined her.

"I don't need my visions to know that something is not right." Morgana's voice was barely above a whisper, "I can at least keep you company, I might even get to cuddle Astra, one last time."

Tahira tilted her head towards Morgana, "I'm not sure that this is the end of the world that you were so concerned about."

"Maybe, maybe not, I am really pleased to say that I don't know. However that's not what I was referring to. Namud is preparing to take his family back to their homeland, they are not fighters they are simple traders." She took a deep breath, "He has asked me to go with him and I said yes."

Tahira smiled and hugged her friend "Good for you, I'm not sure he knows what he has let himself in for mind. I have to say that, in contrast to everyone else round here, our friend Namud has had more of a twinkle in his eye these last few days." She wrapped her arm around Morgana, "Come on then, let's get going."

They arrived at their vantage point at sunrise. Not that they could see it due to the thick fog that covered the sea. Tahira began to imagine a gentle offshore breeze. She thought about it billowing and rolling, pushing and prodding the clouds of mist. She envisioned being able to see a flat calm ocean beneath.

"Not now Tahira, not now, save your strength."

Morgana watched as the ocean mist once more covered an area of the sea that had begun to clear. She was grateful that the breeze that had sprung up from nowhere had ceased. She had felt the wind chill in her bones. She had prepared for a long vigil and so turned her attention to gathering some firewood to boil some water. The wood was damp from the overnight chill and she couldn't light it. Tahira offered to help whilst Morgana searched for drier branches and twigs. She need not have worried. The water was near boiling by the time she came back, the pine needles having infused their sweetness into the clear liquid, "You are a woman of many talents my dear Tahira."

They sipped their tea as the sun began to win its battle with the night. The clouds that had seemed physically attached to the ocean waves were starting to lose their grip. They receded, beginning at the coast. Gradually they revealed the dead calm sea below the headland. It stretched and yawned, dragging the grey miasma back to its source.

They watched and waited. And then they saw a ship, or at least the top mast of a ship, it was hard to make out. It was difficult to judge distance but it was at least a league away. Still the mist slowly crawled away from the promontory. Was that another boat? Where they heading towards the land?

Did they hear a noise? A startled voice carried on the tendrils of air. They heard another shout. There was desperation in it, a wretched call to action.

TAHIRA THE ELEMENTAL

Still the vapours lingered shrouding their contents. The lead ship broke free from its entrapment. They could hear more screams urging the sailors on.

"Aija, that's Elita's ship!" Tahira was shouting.

The second ship now broke free from its cloudy prison. Tahira could see that the second mast was damaged but it was moving forward. The oarsmen where working hard.

They then heard another sound reverberating out across the sea. It was being held in by the misty gloom but it was repetitive. It was a deadened sound but unmistakeable.

"Boom!" The war drum was intended to bring fear. And then they saw the first mast of a Norsemen's war ship through the fog. "Boom!" Then another emerged from its ghostly shroud. "Boom!"

Tahira's blood began to boil. Her heartrate went through the roof as yet more and more warships escaped their hazy shackles. Aija and the other, smaller boat were working hard to keep ahead but they would soon run out of energy and be caught before they reached the harbour. But that was not Tahira's main worry. She watched along with Morgana as a procession of warships emerged from the sea haar. There was over eighty of them.

She looked over to the left and right to check the defences that the Jutes had put in place. She knew, as did the remaining residents of Kobenharven, that they would be no match for the Norsemen's war machine. Some of the defenders began to flee. At this rate the Norsemen would make landfall by midday.

"Look! They have stopped chasing Aija!" Morgana's shout broke Tahira's concentration. Tahira could see that whilst the two Jute boats were heading for the harbour the warships ignored them. They were heading for the beaches south of the headland, the very beaches that they overlooked.

Tahira handed the sleeping Astra to Morgana, "Whatever happens you get her somewhere safe." With that Tahira turned and headed towards the southerly beach, "Go, please, take her back." Tahira pleaded with Morgana who reluctantly did as she was beseeched.

With amazing agility and fleetness of foot Tahira quickly scrambled, ran and rolled her way to the beach. The defenders had all abandoned their positions. The defences they had put in place were ramshackle at best. Wooden spikes driven into the sand would at best only delay the onslaught. There were only enough arrows to take out a quarter of the enemy's combatants assuming that every arrow found its intended target. Tahira couldn't blame the citizens of Kobenharven for running away.

As she looked out to sea the last of the sea haar had cleared. She reflected that on any other winter's day, with the sun rising in the sky and the flat calm sea, that the view would have been amazing. But not today, today the only thing she could see was a mass of warships heading straight for her and the only thing she could hear was the repetitive boom of a drum urging the warriors onwards and towards their prey.

She rubbed her hands to try and bring some warmth to them as her warm breath condensed into vapour.

Then she began to let her anger take control. "Boom!"

She raised her hands. She imagined fireballs crashing into the sides of the great big wooden hulks of Norse warships. "Boom!"

She looked across the ocean, there was no fire. "Boom!"

TAHIRA THE ELEMENTAL

Without stopping she imagined the sea floor and how it would rise and cut through the surface of the ocean blocking the path of the ships. "Boom!"

She looked across the ocean, there were no rocks. "Boom!"

Concerned Tahira switched her train of thought. She imagined a storm of immeasurable power, swirling and seeking out a boat. She imagined lightening smashing bolts of white hot energy into the masts of ships. "Boom!"

Opening her eyes she was distraught to see that there was no tempest. "Boom!"

The war ships were half a league away. "Boom!" Her panic rose. She needed to think. Her previous night's vision came into her head. A frozen fjord trapped in time. "Boom!"

"But I don't know how." Her cry was desperate and was immediately followed by complete and utter silence. Tahira could no longer feel the air around her nor the sand beneath her feet. It was as if she was outside of her body. Time stopped. She felt something ethereal hold her. She felt love. She felt safe.

"*Heat is energy, energy is heat.*" Her inner voice was warm and encouraging, "*When you create fire you add energy, you use your anger to heat something such as wood to such a temperature that it combusts and bursts into flame, similarly when you create a maelstrom you are adding energy to the air through your fear, even grief, the energy you give it allows the air particles to move faster and faster, and when you feel threatened you have learned how to move the earth by changing the state of the energy allowing you to manipulate the particles.*"

Tahira didn't need to ask her next question, her inner voice had already anticipated it, "*Now you need to focus on taking heat away, by removing the energy from water you will force the particles to stop moving, it will give them no choice but to join together, they will crystalize and become solid."*

Tahira imagined but, as she moved the energy from one particle it simply moved into the next making that one warmer.

"You need to move it further way, remember when you added energy to the air you created violent winds and crashing storms, you contained it into a small area, the energy had nowhere else to go, now imagine that you moved the wind much further away, to another land altogether, the added energy goes away and is dispersed and weakened, it is the same now, you simply need to remove the energy and send it away and, it doesn't need to be a great tempest, even a mild breeze will be enough to drive the energy from out of the sea."

Tahira mentally acknowledged and turned to her imagination. She thought about how the air particles just above the ocean waves could become warmer. She dreamt that they would rise up to the clouds where the air currents would take those warmed particles to a land faraway.

"Good, that's good, now imagine it across the whole of the surface of the bay in front of you."

Tahira saw in her mind's eye small clusters of warmed air rising up above the waves. As they did so cooler pockets of energy trapped in the water took their place. She took yet more heat out of the sea water and used it to warm that cooler air. It too began to rise. She watched as cloud after cloud began drifting away on some higher air current.

She was now standing on the beach staring at the waves, they had stopped moving. The surface of the water was coloured white. She took a step forward, trusting it to take her weight. It was cold and hard as stone. As she looked further out to sea so she saw the pack ice moving at pace towards the war ships of the Norsemen. She confidently took another step. As she moved closer to the lead ship she watched as the sea froze solid all around each vessel. They were stuck unable to move despite the power of the oarsmen. The wooden hulls began to creak and groan. The ice was expanding, rising and crushing anything it encased. All the time Tahira imagined warm air rising, from the top of the water and ice, only to be swept way.

As she approached the first ship the port side succumbed to the pressure from the ice. The large timbers splintered into matchsticks. Then she saw the dreaded Norsemen for the first time. They were shouting and screaming at each other but she could hear no sound. She couldn't be sure if they could see her.

She imagined another boat with its deck smashed beyond repair and then another. She moved around the ice freely as if in a dream. For the Norsemen this was no dream only a nightmare as each boat felt the strength of the expanding ice. For some it was more catastrophic than others.

Tahira watched amazed as some unknown signal commanded the surviving sailors to leave their stricken ships. They quickly gathered their weapons and began to march towards the beach and the safety of landfall. She moved silently and deftly to be in front of them. It was an impressive sight as several hundred men moved as one.

She arrived on the beach two hundred paces ahead of them. She turned to face the warrior horde. Then Tahira imagined what it would be like to take the warm air and move it towards the ice. She thought about how the ice might begin to melt as the heat from the midday sun might force the icy bonds apart freeing the particles to move as they saw fit. She saw the pack ice begin to break apart. Large icebergs slowly drifted on the now exposed surface of the ocean.

She saw the thinning ice beneath the warriors fragment unable to sustain the weight. At first just a few of the men succumbed to their watery grave. But soon the domino effect took over as the masses of fighting men desperately fought for air, arms frantically splashing the water but to no avail.

Tahira imagined hundreds of pairs of hands reaching up through the surface of the water in a futile attempt to escape their fate. She looked down at these disembodied hands and felt nothing. The numbers dwindled and the sea returned to the stillness of a millpond.

She looked out to sea. Over half of the warships had sunk without a trace. Of those that were left most would need repair but it was of no concern to Tahira.

She looked across the ocean towards Kobenharven harbour. There she could see a damaged vessel next to a ship she recognised as Aija. They had been unaffected. She could see sailors waving their hands and cheering. Tahira smiled as she turned her gaze back to the fleet of stricken warships. The once might army of Norsemen now lying at the bottom of the sea.

It was then that she felt the gentle breeze brush her cheek, she thought she heard bird song, she felt exhaustion overwhelm her. Tahira blacked out.

"Rest now, my child. We love you."

A Royal Coronation

Tahira could hear the women's voices. She felt they were close. They were familiar and reassuring. She slowly opened her eyes. She was comforted to see Morgana, Elita, Jasmina and another woman who she did not recognise. Jasmina was holding Astra close to her bosom. Closing her eyes again she focused, the whispered words were reassuring.

Tahira recalled seeing the fighting ships of the Norsemen and the fear and loathing it instilled in both herself and the Jutes. She was distraught at the fact that she had been responsible for the deaths of all those men but what option did she have? Elita's father had tried diplomacy which had clearly failed, she couldn't let them subjugate, enslave or worse still kill Elita's countrymen. Where would it have stopped if she hadn't taken such drastic action?

In her short life all she had experienced was Man's greed for wealth and power, it appeared limitless to her.

Her inner thoughts were broken by the sound of Elita sobbing. Jasmina comforted her.

"Oh it's OK, Jasmina, I just need a minute. I'll be alright." Elita sniffed.

Jasmina, who had been breastfeeding Astra, passed Tahira's daughter over to Elita, "Just look into those eyes, they will make you feel better, it's like magic."

Tahira had watched the mini spectacle unseen by her friends, "Maybe I could do with some of that magic as well," Her voice was soft, "and a pine tea would be nice, if there's one on the go?"

Elita and Jasmina rushed over to Tahira with Astra. There were lots of hugs. Morgana brought the tea. Tahira looked into Astra's eyes and melted, "Yep they're magic alright." She cuddled her smiling daughter.

The other lady who Tahira did not recognise was an older grey haired woman. She stood at the end of the bed patiently waiting her turn to be formally introduced, which eventually Elita did, after the lady had 'cleared her throat ' a couple of times to attract her attention.

Nawali bowed her head before she spoke with a heavily accented but warm voice. She addressed Tahira formally, "My Lady Tahira, on behalf of the people of Juteria, I Queen Nawali would like to confer our profound thanks and gratitude for all you have done for my people, without you, we would be lost to those Norse devils."

"Mother, please, I told you." Elita made her irritation known.

"Shush, someone has to."

"Not now Mother, please."

"Look, Elita, Queen Nawali." Tahira raised her hand, "Your thanks are appreciated, but I am not sure what you saw or heard."

Jasmina couldn't resist and jumped in, "Well my Lady Tahira, from Aija we could see you on the beach with your arms raised, it got cold, so cold that the water began to freeze, you walked on it and all the men on the warships got out and began to march to the land following you but they never made it. As quickly as the ice came so it disappeared taking all the Norsemen with it."

"Oh yes, I remember now, we got very lucky didn't we?"

TAHIRA THE ELEMENTAL

Jasmina was about to interrupt again before Morgana quickly and softly kicked her in the shin. "You must be hungry Tahira? You have been sleeping for over three days." She turned to the others, "She could also do with some quiet as well, don't you think?"

Nawali smiled, "Of course, come my daughter, we must make preparations." Although reluctant to leave they knew it was for the best.

Tahira laid Astra in her cot before she began to pick at her food, it was however enough to make her feel better. As Morgana cleared away the plate she asked, "What are they making preparations for?"

"They are going to select their new king." Morgana answered.

"What?" Tahira was shocked. "I think someone needs to tell me what has happened in my absence."

Morgana refilled Tahira's cup and sat herself down in the chair next to Tahira's bed.

"Well I am sure that I don't know all the details but, before I start I think you should know that I saw what you did. Now you can try to claim that it was a miracle about how the ice came and all that but I know different. You are a very special young lady with powers that I cannot comprehend. I watched you bring forth the ice sheet, I saw you ride an iceberg on top of it, I heard the ships being crushed as you approached them. With my own eyes I gazed in disbelief at all those warriors as they began to march towards the land with you leading them, and, I stared in awe when you turned to face the horde and with a wave of your hand melted the ice away."

"You didn't go back to camp then?"

"I couldn't Tahira and it's just as well. Someone had to carry you back here."

"Well, in that case, I am glad that you didn't listen to me then." Tahira smiled.

Morgana waved her gratitude away, "Well to be honest it was Astra's doing, she cried and cried until I took her back towards the beach. As soon as we could see you she stopped crying. She then waved her arms mirroring your actions, I placed her on the ground and tried to call to you but you appeared to be in a trance or something. Then, when I looked back at Astra she too appeared to be in a similar state. It was as if you were both locked together. After it was over you slumped to the ground but Astra just smiled and clapped her hands." She paused briefly, "I don't know how I managed to carry both you and Astra back here, I have no memory of doing it, I bent down to pick up Astra who gave me a great big cuddle and the next thing I know I am here and you are in bed fast sleep."

"Astra magic?" offered Tahira.

"Well she is your daughter after all, my Lady Tahira!" Morgana smiled, "Now you must rest, I'm sure Jasmina will be here in a few hours to continue with her wet nurse duties."

Tahira didn't try to counter Morgana's story. Jasmina and Elita, along with the crews of Aija and the other damaged Juterian ship must have seen what happened. Even if they were further away, they could still speculate. Jasmina had seen what Tahira had done to King Olenus's ships. Elita had suspected there was more to the flaming arrow story when defeating the pirates of the Franecian coast. There seemed little point in trying to hide who, or what, she was. If only she knew herself.

TAHIRA THE ELEMENTAL

"I am more comfortable talking about other people, so, tell me why are they selecting a new king? I take it that it isn't good news?"

Morgana smiled, for years she had carried the mantle of being special, even cursed, as seen by others. She had worn it with a heavy heart particularly when her visions had shown news that her patrons hadn't wanted to hear. She could only guess at the power that the young woman in front of her held. And, she could only imagine the emotional turmoil that she had to go through when she used her gifts. This young girl had brought life into this world but had also taken it away, hundreds of souls where now languishing at the bottom of the ocean as a result of her actions. She had to concede though that her talents had saved the lives of countless thousands of other people, including her own and those of her new family. It was a cross she was glad she did not have to bear.

"My understanding is that there was a lot of discussion but Elita's brother insisted that he lead the delegation to find their father. Aija was to act as a rear guard. As they approached the coast of Skandia, the land of the Norsemen, they were given a four boat escort and ordered to sail toward a nearby headland and cove. It was a carefully laid trap. The Jutes were not expecting to see so many ships. They were also not expecting to see their King tied to the prow of the Norsemen's lead battleship. The drums sounded and the warships headed for their prey. The Juterian ships couldn't readily manoeuver out of the way due to the Norse ships that flanked them. Elita could hear the sound of the lead ship crash into her brother's smaller vessel."

"But wasn't her father tied to the front of the Norse ship?" Tahira was alarmed.

"He was, and, he was still alive."

Tahira involuntarily placed her hand over her mouth. A tear rolled down her cheek.

Morgana continued, "The Norse warships were nearly twice as big as the Juterian boats. They didn't stand a chance. Four of the leading vessels where smashed in the first attack. Knowing that they were outnumbered they desperately tried to retreat. In the chaos and carnage the remaining Juterian boats managed to escape the blockade. Aija being smaller, more nimble and with a better trained crew, took the lead as night fell. It gave them some breathing space, as did the settling fog but, throughout the night Elita could hear one Juterian ship at a time being picked off and sent to a watery grave, each one another dagger to her heart. There was nothing they could do but to retreat and hope. As the mists lifted they saw you and it gave them that hope. Of the thirteen Juterian ships that left to rescue their King only two made it out alive, and, for that Elita also feels guilty. Other than her Mother she has lost her whole family."

Tahira cried yet more tears, "And then?"

"Well, they had the formal funeral for all the Juterian men and women that lost their lives in the fight with the Norsemen. The ship that returned with Aija was very badly damaged with its captain having been killed in action. It was decided that he should represent all the lost souls with the ship symbolising the lost vessels. As such it was taken out of the harbour and set alight as the people of Kobenharven and surrounding villages grieved their collective loss."

TAHIRA THE ELEMENTAL

"That's a fitting tribute." Tahira dried her eyes, "So that would leave Elita's mother, Queen Nawali as the new head of state, yes?"

"Sadly no, Juterian society doesn't quite work that way. Word travels fast and a tribal leader from the other side of the land has claimed that he is the rightful King of the Jutes. There is a meeting in the morning to formally agree the handover process." Morgana plumped up Tahira's pillow, "Anyway that's enough now, time for some more rest before Jasmina gets here and feeds Astra."

In the morning Tahira, shrouded in her cape, strode confidently into the town looking for her friends Elita and Jasmina. Astra gurgled happily safe and warm in the papoose sling that Morgana had made for her mother. She found Jasmina at the harbour orchestrating the final repairs to Aija.

"I missed you this morning. I wanted to thank you for feeding little Astra for me." Tahira hugged her friend.

"Not a problem. In fact it was a pleasure. It gave me a perfect excuse to have plenty of cuddles." Jasmina quickly turned to one of Aija's crew and barked an order at him.

"I see that being one of the captain's favourites has its benefits?" Tahira laughed.

"Oh I'm just keeping myself occupied whilst Elita and her mother organise the selection of the new King. They've just started."

"Where is it taking place exactly? Can you spare a few minutes and take me there?"

"No need." Jasmina pointed her finger to a large ornate structure. It was the only stone building in the town and overlooked the harbour. Tahira set off.

Jasmina desperately tried to catch up with her friend, "You can't go in there, it's a private meeting."

It was no use. The guard on the door quickly stepped aside. He had heard of Tahira's reputation and decided that today cowardice was his best form of valour.

Tahira entered a large meeting hall. At the far end was a small round table. On one side sat Queen Nawali and Elita. Opposite was a small entourage of men dressed in fancy robes. One of these nobles was standing and clearly didn't appreciate being interrupted.

"Oh don't mind me, my name is Tahira and this here is my friend Jasmina." Tahira waved her hand as she sat next to Queen Nawali with Jasmina nervously taking the vacant seat next to Elita.

The middle aged man smiled, "My dear Lady Tahira, it is both an honour and a privilege to meet you." He stiffly stood to attention and bowed, as did each member of his support staff. He waited for them to return to their seats before continuing, "Let me introduce myself, my name is Sigurd," there was a small cough from a tall thin man with a grey beard who was sitting directly opposite Tahira, "Oh yes, please excuse me, King Sigurd."

Tahira smiled her acknowledgement.

"For the record I would like it known that in recognition of the great service you have given to my people that I, King Sigurd, will present you with our highest civilian award at my coronation. I will also give you one hundred gold coins from the treasury in gratitude." King Sigurd beamed a big smile.

"My dear sir, the gratitude of the Juterian people is more than enough for me, I do not need nor want your money, I would rather that was spent wisely providing a pension to the families that have recently lost their fathers, brothers and sons in the futile war with the armies of Skandia."

King Sigurd looked at the tall thin man who nodded, "You teach me a great lesson, my lady. We will indeed make provision for all those people that suffered a loss in the recent battle with the Norsemen. We will also avenge them."

"Avenge them Sir, how? They have lost countless warriors along with eighty or so of their warships. Half of which you have dragged into the harbour and will repair no doubt."

"My dear Lady, as soon as we repair and train our young men we will exact a bloody revenge against our enemy and wipe the vile Norsemen from the history books. We will strike them whilst they are weak, thanks to you." Sigurd spat the last words out.

Tahira could feel the anger swell inside her, "How many wars have YOU fought? How many men did YOU lose to the Norsemen?"

"My men were ready to fight!" Sigurd was losing his composure.

"The people of Kobenharven lost hundreds of men whilst you sat of your fat backsides. You did nothing but plot and scheme. You are not fit to be a King!" Tahira voice was loud and commanding. She hadn't lost her temper, not yet. Sigurd was breathless, how dare this young girl, and a foreigner at that, talk to him that way but before he could respond Tahira continued, "The people of Juteria deserve better. I suggest that you show fealty to Queen Nawali instead and to your future head of state Princess Elita."

A shout rang out, "Never!" It came from a tall, thin man sitting opposite Tahira. He banged the table with his fist as he stood up. He was well over six feet in length with weasel like facial features. He raised his finger at Queen Nawali, "That is Persean scum and that," he then pointed his finger in Elita's direction, "is a half breed."

"Sit down Gustav." King Sigurd commanded his aide. He desperately wanted to regain control of the situation.

Tahira looked across at her friends, they showed no emotion. They stared expressionless almost hypnotised. Her anger grew more, underneath her cloak she reached for the cold hard metal of her throwing knives. Her subconscious mind worked out the distances between her and each of her intended targets. There were only five of them. It would be over in a matter of seconds. She had killed hundreds of men before and adding a few more to her list would not bother her in the slightest.

"No." Elita's voice was calm and measured. She had moved quickly, almost sensing what was going on in Tahira's mind. She was standing next to her, "Please, if not for me then for my people."

Tahira was confused. Astra wriggled and looked into her mother's eyes. Her anger dissipated. She placed the first two knives back in their holder. Elita kissed her gently on the cheek and whispered, "Thank you."

King Sigurd, who remained unaware how close he had come to the end of his life, requested a quick recess to gather their thoughts. They soon departed with Sigurd mumbling quietly at his party of advisors.

TAHIRA THE ELEMENTAL

"Bless you Tahira but you don't understand," Queen Nawali broke the silence, "My husband broke all the Juterian rules when he married me, he fought several battles against other clan leaders including Sigurd's father, many people lost their lives because of his love for me."

"I have known since birth that women cannot lead the Jutes. I wasn't happy about it and I fought my brothers like crazy to prove I was a match for them." Elita had now taken over, "Anyway, the last thing I want to do is to be here. If I stayed I would be married off to some stupid man, that's why I ran away to begin with, I love being a trader and having the life on the high seas, and even more so now." She turned towards Jasmina and held her hand.

Tahira was slightly taken aback, even more so when Queen Nawali said, "Oh don't worry dear, I've known for years, although I must admit it took me a bit longer to work it out than you did." She smiled, "Besides, I want to go and see my sister who still lives in Susa, Namud and Morgana have offered to take me at least part of the way, I will be staying with them at Namud's homestead for the rest of the winter, we'll be leaving in a few days before the snows come."

"Did you know this?" Tahira looked quizzically at Jasmina,

"Well yes, but you never gave me chance to tell you before you came in here with your big mouth, and big feet." She smiled and disarmed Tahira in the process.

"Right, looks like I made a bit of a fool of myself then." Tahira was slightly embarrassed.

"No not at all. Erm, I hope you don't mind, the door was open." A rather hesitant young man barely older than Tahira had made his way back into the hall. "My Father asked me to come and see if it would be possible to reconvene in a few moments. My name is Sigurdsson."

Tahira recognised him as one of her previously intended targets. He quickly averted his eyes when they made contact with hers. His beard was wispy and light brown. His light complexion offset by piercing blue eyes.

"That would be acceptable Sigurdsson, sorry beg your forgiveness, Prince Sigurdsson." Queen Nawali had stepped forward.

The King's company returned minus Gustav. "My dear Queen Nawali, please accept my humble apologies for the behaviour of certain members of my advisory panel, they have been punished accordingly."

Queen Nawali expressed her gratitude before welcoming King Sigurd to speak further. Tahira determined to listen and to hold her tongue.

"We are grateful to yourself and your daughter for agreeing to step aside in accordance with our laws. We have also taken the time to access Lady Tahira's observations. We would like to formally declare that the people of Juteria will not seek further retribution from the Norse people. We accept that they too have suffered enough from the battle between our peoples. We will however repair their warships for defensive purposes only. The offer of a pension to the affected families will remain. I trust this is acceptable to you? You have my word on it." He didn't move his eyes away from Queen Nawali who readily accepted his assurances.

They spent another hour or so further discussing the handover process. The coronation itself would be held the following day before he embarked on a tour of his new

TAHIRA THE ELEMENTAL

kingdom. He expected that to take the rest of the winter with the view that he would move his court to Kobenharven at the start of summer.

Tahira found it hard to remain awake by the end of the meeting, stifling many a yawn. Astra slept peacefully.

At the end of the meeting Queen Nawali offered to show King Sigurd around the civic building as well as the large wooden fort and palace that would become his new home.

Tahira needed some fresh air for no better reason than to keep herself awake. Outside the winter sun tried its best to warm the day. She crossed the square and stood at the edge of the tidal waters.

"I hope you don't mind me asking but would you really have killed us all, my Lady Tahira?" Sigurdsson spoke with a measure to his voice that belied his youthfulness.

Tahira turned to face the young man. This time he did not immediately avert his eyes when they met hers. He bowed gracefully. He offered her a cup carved out of soapstone. In which was a hot brown liquid. The vapours condensed as they met the frigid air.

Tahira was hesitant, even guarded.

"Try it, it is safe to drink." He took a sip from his own cup.

"Nice, what is it?" Tahira was pleasantly surprised. It was an unusual but pleasing flavour.

"We call it Kaffa, it's made from chicory root with a spoonful of honey to take away some of the bitterness." He paused briefly, "It will also keep you awake during boring meetings." Sigurdsson smiled.

"In which case I thank you." Tahira paused thoughtfully, "To answer your question, yes I would. I would do everything in my power to defend my family and friends."

"I appreciate your candour, good lady. I have heard tales of the Dogon throwing knives but I have only seen them in a book." He noted Tahira's quizzical look, "Oh I caught a glimpse of you holding one in your right hand through a small gap in your cape."

"Well I was more surprised about you referring to a book. In my experience noblemen rarely look at books, especially the young men. Aren't you supposed to focus on fighting and hunting?"

"But how else are we to learn? I learnt all my military strategy through reading. My books showed me what weapons are best in certain situations. In them I've seen weapons, such as the throwing knives, which our people have never even heard off, let alone used."

Tahira interrupted, "It is still all about fighting."

"No. Not at all, my lady!" Prince Sigurdsson jumped in clearly excited. He then thought for a moment before continuing, "That is but one book. I have others, in fact I have more than anyone else in the kingdom combined. Each page is filled with works of science, medicine and poetry. Others tell tales of myths and legends. They cover all the wonders that this world has to offer. I have some with me I could show you, if you like?"

Tahira noted the sparkle in his eyes.

"Oh there you are. Are you still talking to me then?" Elita broke Tahira's train of thought.

TAHIRA THE ELEMENTAL

She laughed in response, "Of course, I will never stop talking to you."

Jasmina offered to feed Astra.

"Oh you have a child, my lady Tahira. I did not know that you were married." Prince Sigurdsson blurted out his apology and began to back away.

Jasmina stopped him in his tracks and held Astra out for him to hold. Without flinching he cradled Astra in his muscled arm. For her part she smiled and in common with everyone else his heart melted before he quickly felt acute embarrassment and gave Astra back to Jasmina. As the three women resumed their conversation Sigurdsson slipped quietly away.

Leaving Elita and Jasmina to work on repairing their trading vessel Aija, Tahira made her way back to Namud's camp. Under Morgana's strict orders she rested for the remainder of the day. Despite the cold evening Namud's family group ate their evening meal around the camp fire before returning to their tents to sleep. They would be leaving as soon as the coronation was over.

Morgana placed Astra into her crib and gently rocked her to sleep as Tahira washed her face.

"You could always come with us, Tahira. Namud would not object."

"My dear Morgana, I would love that but, I need to go home, I promised Amir to meet him back in Atlassia on the first day of summer, he needs to meet his beautiful daughter."

"I know," Morgana sighed, "but I am going to miss you and Astra."

"And I will miss you terribly, I owe you so much, but rest assured we will come and find you, you have my word on it."

"It's just..."

"Are your visions back?"

"Oh no, it's not that! I can't quite put my finger on it. Call it intuition if you want but I can't help feeling that this isn't over yet, and I am worried about you."

"If it helps I haven't had any of those visions, not since the Norsemen drowned." Tahira wasn't happy to lie to her friend but felt that it would be better for Morgana.

With Astra settled Morgana leant over and kissed Tahira on the forehead. "When did you get the yellow crystal for your amulet, it looks beautiful?"

Without thinking Tahira reached for her necklace and held it aloft. She could see the flickering firelight dance through the thin sheets of multi-coloured crystal. The gift her unknown Mother had given her was truly beautiful. The red garnet, green emerald and blue azurite crystals had now been joined and complemented by a stunning and vibrant yellow citrine. She drifted off to sleep clutching her amulet.

The next morning's coronation of King Sigurd was a rather quiet, even subdued affair. The vast majority of the town's folk did their civic duty and lined the main square at the dockside and watched politely as a small gold crown was placed upon King Sigurd's head by Queen Nawali.

King Sigurd's acceptance speech mirrored the previous day's agreement. The offer of a pension to the families affected by the recent battle with the Norsemen was warmly applauded. After which the crowd dissipated and went back to their everyday lives.

TAHIRA THE ELEMENTAL

By midday Kobenharven had returned to normal. The sounds and the smells of the docks were as they were before the recent events had sullied the memories of its inhabitants.

"Permission to come aboard Captain?" Tahira had already placed one foot on the gang plank leading to Aija.

"Your request is granted but only if you have brought that darling daughter of yours with you." Elita sounded more like her old self. Astra was freed from her papoose and handed to both the Pirate Queen and her Princess.

"Didn't see you at the coronation?" Tahira said as she followed them to their quarters.

"No, I made myself unavailable, besides I wanted to get the crew ready to begin loading a cargo of skins and whale oil. We are sailing to Franecia on tomorrow's high tide. Once my mother leaves later today there is nothing left for me here. Would you like to come with us or are you travelling back with Morgana?" Elita and Jasmina were looking hopefully at Tahira.

"Well," began Tahira hesitantly, "I promised to meet Amir back in Atlassia at the start of the summer and if I go back with Morgana I won't make it so travelling with my friends on Aija would be very much appreciated, I will obviously pay my way and sleep out on the deck."

Elita laughed, "Absolutely no chance, just having little Astra on board will be payment enough, no offence!"

Tahira had hoped that Elita might be in need of getting away from her home town for a while. Travelling by ship was certainly going to prove quicker than horse and far more comfortable. She began helping the crew load their cargo before Elita realised what she was doing and ordered her away until the following day.

It was late afternoon as Tahira made her way across the town square towards the main civic building and the palace beyond. She had previously arranged to meet up with Queen Nawali and escort her to Namud's camp. Once at the palace she was advised that the queen was as usual running late.

"Don't suppose you've got any more of that kaffa have you?" Tahira placed her washed but empty stone cup on the small desk next to the book Sigurdsson was reading. She had been wandering the civic rooms killing time when she found the small anteroom which housed a few precious books on its shelves. Sigurdsson had been completely oblivious to her presence.

He was a little startled, "My Lady Tahira. I did not hear you come in. I am sorry!" He stood up.

Tahira laughed, "My dear Prince Sigurdsson there is nothing for you to apologise for, and please, it's just Tahira. So what are you reading?"

"Oh it's amazing, look." He pointed to a section of the book. There were a couple of hand drawn images of creatures she did not recognise. Using his finger as a guide he read the word underneath one of the pictures, "Dinosauri, I have never heard of such a creature, and look here" He excitedly opened the first page of the book. It contained a drawing of a land she did not know, "It's a map of a land called Antarti, which can be found at the very bottom of the world, it would take a year to sail there apparently, I would love to go there, wouldn't you?"

Tahira nodded her agreement, "It sounds amazing, have you travelled much before?"

"Sadly no, only in my books, I have heard and read tales about people whose skin has a different colour to ours, of giants that live in caves in the far East that have bodies covered in fur, did you know there are little people, no bigger than a child who live in a land where you cannot see the sky for the giant leaves on incredibly tall trees? By reading books I can live a thousand lives."

Tahira sat on the bench next to him. She placed her hand on his. He stopped speaking and blushed before using that hand to turn the next page in the book more awkwardly than he had expected.

"I speak several languages but I cannot read, would you be kind enough to teach me." Tahira looked into Sigurdsson's eyes. They appeared to sparkle the more he spoke about his precious books.

"I would love to my lady but, it would take a long time. Sadly I have to leave with my father tomorrow on our Grand Tour of his Kingdom." He paused thoughtfully as he looked into Tahira's eyes, "You are not like any other woman I have ever met." He hesitated, "Can you keep a secret Tahira? I don't want to be king, my older sister would be much better at ruling than me."

"Well why don't you plant that seed? He obviously listened to you yesterday."

"Yes but that was easy really, Gustav really embarrassed him. My father is many things but he is an absolute stickler for protocol. Your suggestion regarding the setting up of a pension for the families that suffered a loss helped alleviate his perceived humiliation. Remember he had previously earmarked that money as a payment to you. If you hadn't done what you did, whatever that was, he would never have become King of the Jutes. As for not waging war on the Norse that was even easier, wars cost money. We don't have that much gold and the Norse have even less. They lost their entire fleet on warships in one day, can you imagine how much gold they would need to replace them." He paused as he theatrically tapped the open book on the desk, "One of the advantages of reading is the knowledge that it gives and he appreciates that so he listened to my arguments."

Tahira was increasingly impressed by this young man. "Well I still think you should drop a few hints along with arguments for and against, maybe the Juterian people need to change. After all it was an ordinary woman that defeated the Norse army!"

"My Lady Tahira," Sigurdsson pointedly remarked, "You'll forgive me for saying this but you are no ordinary woman." His level of confidence dropped again whilst his face flushed red. He reached into a small bag at his feet and pulled out a small leather bound book, "My grandmother gave me this book when I was a young boy. It reminds me of her and the hours of fun we had, it is my most treasured possession. Now the first thing to note is that most books are written in Celtic which is the language of trade after all. Being a Celt gives you a distinct advantage over people like me because I am a native Juterian speaker."

He opened the first page. Tahira recognised the drawing of an apple with a word underneath and a big letter on top of the page. The next page was in a similar format but with a picture of a bee. "Oh is this an alphabet book? My friend Jamilah uses something similar to teach the young children in Atlassia, the capital city of Atlantea."

"Atlantea? You know of the people of Atlantea, a hot dry land full of sand?"

"It's my home, well my new home."

"You must tell me more."

"Not now my dear Prince Sigurdsson, first you are teaching me how to read."

He was shaking his head, "One day I would love to go and visit." He pointed to the picture in the book and the letters and began to sound the letters out to create the word.

Tahira listened intently. She had seen books before and had a vague memory of her father sitting with her reading stories from a parchment when she was very small. She remembered how Amir would sit hunched over scrolls with various writings on them, he even wrote words on clay tablets. She closed her eyes and listened to the voice of her tutor. He created stories to explain each word. In her mind she saw the images with the sentences written out beneath them. The words were warm and comforting.

"Ah there you are my dear Tahira." Queen Nawali's voice broke her reverie. She bowed, "Prince Sigurdsson, I do apologise, I didn't realise."

"That's no problem, Queen Nawali. We were just talking and reading." Sigurdsson rose as he stammered his words out, "I must go anyway, I need to prepare for my father's trip in the morning. Good day Queen Nawali." he turned and bowed to Tahira, "My Lady."

As he left Queen Nawali looked at Tahira, "I hope I wasn't disturbing anything?" She beamed a great big smile at Astra who giggled in response.

Tahira was now standing and looped her arm in Queen Nawali's, "Come on let's get you up to camp. When was the last time you slept in a tent my Queen?"

"Don't remind me, it's been at least thirty years. But, it's all part of my new adventure now." She paused briefly, "Oh and it's just Nawali now. I must admit that I am looking forward to stopping the pretence and formality associated with being a Juterian Queen."

Tahira helped her new friend up and onto the front seat of her cart. It looked like any other trading cart, even the horse pulling it looked a bit down trodden. Nawali had done her research and embraced this new lifestyle, at least for now. The driver was the only person from her retinue to remain with her. Tahira was introduced to Zirak, a tall, handsome man of Persean origin. He appeared to be of a similar age to Nawali. Tahira saw something in his eyes that reminded her of Elita.

Tahira hoisted herself into the back of the cart which was heavily laden with all manner of goods. "We've brought some things to sell along the way." Nawali was feeling pleased with herself.

As was the usual practice Astra was handed around to everyone in Namud's camp. It was almost ritualistic. The precious moments of joy she brought into the lives of everyone who gazed into those mesmerising eyes had an addictive quality. Even grumpy old Namud was bewitched by her. The fact that it was to be their last opportunity made it all the more poignant.

The morning was greeted by the first wispy snowfall of winter, just enough to cover the ground in a white powdery blanket. The air remained chill, even after the sun had fully risen above the horizon. To the north Tahira could see clouds building in the distance. They were being carried on a very gentle breeze but once they arrived the snow would fall for several days. The timing of Morgana and Nawali's departure could not be better. They said their reluctant goodbyes and she watched as they trundled off into the distance, heading south and to warmer climes.

Namud tried to give her some coins for the horses but once again he was met with a flat refusal. She also rejected his offer of a tent and other items that she had borrowed over the last few weeks.

With Astra securely strapped to her chest and with her cape pulled tight, Tahira picked up her back pack and headed back into Kobenharven to begin her own journey south and to the arms of Amir.

The town itself seemed quieter, more subdued. The town's folk were milling about as she had become accustomed to seeing but they appeared sullen and lethargic. Elita shrugged it off as typical for the time of year. "Soon everyone will be hunkered down in their houses and only occasionally venturing outside when the need arises. Come on, we'll be leaving shortly."

It wasn't long before Tahira felt the tell-tale rocking motion on board Aija indicating that she was free from the mud that had encased her hull. "So, did you see your new king depart this morning?"

Elita knew that Tahira was teasing her so she didn't rise to the bait. "Well, we heard them departing first thing this morning. There was plenty of shouting not long after sunrise followed by the entire entourage stomping through the town on their horses. The click clack of the horseshoes on the cobble stones sounded like rhythmical thunder." She paused, "Oh and that handsome young man, Prince Sigurdsson, left you a parcel before he departed. I've put it next to the bed and crib in your quarters."

Tahira was confused. Elita explained that she had got her men to install a privacy panel in the captain's quarters for her. "I was fed up looking at their bits and pieces so I had previously got them to add panels to the latrine area, it was a similar process."

As the high tide reached its peak Elita issued her orders and her crew untied Aija from the dock and raised her anchor. With the gentle off shore breeze to guide her she serenely left the safe harbour of Kobenharven and ventured out, once more, into the open ocean.

A Second Homecoming

They headed north keeping sight of the Juterian coastline on their port side. By early evening they were hit by a major snowstorm. They sought some respite in a sheltered cove. It suited Elita and her crew. They rarely travelled at night unless they absolutely had to.

The girls settled in Elita's cabin and chatted while they drank tea.

"So what did your new friend the handsome Prince Sigurdsson give you?" Elita teased.

Tahira confessed that she hadn't even opened it. Jasmina fetched it before she could move. She handed the package over to Tahira in exchange for a cuddle with Astra.

Her parcel included the stone cup and a pack of chicory root and a jar of honey, "Kaffa, have you tried it? It's a bit different but I quite like it." Elita had heard of it but never tried it. Jasmina shook her head. "Also there are a couple of books, look this one is an alphabet book, it helps you learn to read. His grandmother gave it to him when she taught him to read." She suddenly felt very humbled. She knew it was his most treasured possession but he had given it to her, to help with her reading. Little did he know that following her overnight dreams she was now fully able to read and write in Celta.

"Could you teach me?" Jasmina looked sheepish, even embarrassed.

Elita quickly picked up on her discomfort, "And me Tahira? I can work my way around a map and I have memorised place names."

Her friends had simply assumed that she could read, so she readily agreed to help them. It would certainly make their journey go a bit quicker.

Tahira lifted out a large brown leather backed book. It had exquisite patterns embossed on it in painted gold. She pointed to the title which simply read 'The World'. She recognised it as the book that Sigurdsson had been reading when she saw him the previous day. She enthusiastically showed Elita and Jasmina the page showing the land of Antarti and its animals. Their lessons had begun.

When they woke the weather had eased sufficiently for them to raise the anchor and make sail. Elita expected that they would soon be turning east keeping the land on their port side.

The days were long and Jasmina had not yet really found her place within the crew. Consequently she had a bit more free time than Elita. She was therefore grateful to have Tahira around. Jasmina revelled in learning to read. She found some blank parchment in the bottom of an old trunk. She started drawing the land as she saw it. They were more accurate than the maps Elita was using. In fact they could be used to chart their progress. With Tahira's support and guidance she began to add place names to certain features, including visible sandbanks, rocky outcrops and the like.

When travelling with Tahira through Mycenea and Agathryia Jasmina had been taught about handling weapons. For firing arrows and throwing knives it was critical to know how far your target was away from you. Tahira was exceptional at this but Jasmina was a very able student. She was more than capable of holding her own in a judging distance competition. During some down time she puzzled the crew members by

TAHIRA THE ELEMENTAL

sending arrows, attached to thin rope, hurtling out towards the coastline. They watched bemused as each one fell short of the land. They didn't appreciate that they were falling short by a regular and proportionate amount as indicated by the regular marks of the rope.

They made good and steady progress until twilight when they began to feel the wind chill their bones and so they headed landward for some safety from the coming snowstorm. Fortunately it soon cleared to leave a stunningly beautiful but bitterly cold moonless night sky. With a hot kaffa in her hand and a sleeping Astra in her cot Tahira walked the deck. Most of the crew had retired below decks to escape the cold but Tahira's cape kept her warm. She looked up to the heavens and said a quick hello to her favourite star which seemed to sparkle brighter in response. She bowed her head toward the ever present polestar and tried to imagine what those different worlds would look like.

In her dreams that night she saw long lengths of hemp rope knotted at regular intervals trailing behind Aija. She mentioned it to Jasmina over breakfast. Jasmina reasoned that if you could use the marked rope to measure distance, as they had done with the arrows the previous day then could you use the same principle to work out how fast you are moving. They spent some time discussing how this could work.

Jasmina, once her morning duties were complete, set to work. As Aija moved forward she rolled out a length of rope from the stern. The end in the water had been tied to a piece of wood to keep it afloat. The rope itself had been divided up into regular lengths and marked with a knot. She watched as the ocean took the buoyant wood away pulling even more rope out. By counting the number of knots taken she could estimate the speed. She repeated this process several times and came to realise that each attempt gave her different results.

Whilst having a break with her friends Jasmina voiced her frustrations. Elita tried to calm her down, "It's OK, just give it time. Keep repeating your experiments and you'll get there."

"Of course..." Jasmina exclaimed, "To work out how fast we are moving I need to measure the distance against time. I've been counting the knots as I let them out but what if my counting is not constant?" She fell silent for a while.

"I seem to remember back in Atlassia someone complaining about a constant drip coming from a water pump. An engineer had to replace a piece of worn leather that had been used to help seal a clay pipe." Tahira was thoughtful, "Could we put seawater into one of the goatskins we use to collect freshwater and put a tiny hole in it. It won't last long but it should come out at an even rate."

Jasmina smiled as she left them. She spent the rest of the afternoon working hard. Through trial and error and many repeated attempts Jasmina began to see patterns in her measurements. By the end of the day she had worked out roughly how fast Aija had been moving and could therefore estimate how far they had travelled. "So by my calculations we have travelled six leagues today." She made a note of the distance on her new map.

They were now heading south and progress was good. The reading lessons were also positive with some of the crew also taking part. The following days fell into a steady pattern of activity. The crew were well drilled and happy in their work. Elita was the captain and had the final say on all matters affecting the ship and her crew. However, all the crew benefitted equally from the profits of their trading exploits.

It took them several days to reach their destination port in Franecia. Tahira didn't tell her friends that the dreams and visions which had previously haunted her had returned. She knew she had to find Amir and was desperate to get back to Atlassia. Time, however, was not on her side.

They arrived at the Franecian port as planned. It was familiar to Tahira. It wasn't that long ago that she had arrived here but so much had changed in the last year or so of her life. As they entered the river estuary they were carefully watched by the militia men in the tower that guarded the entrance.

As they approached the dock itself, a score of heavily armed men greeted them. The officer in charge shouted at them in Celta, "State your place of departure and nature of your business." Elita looked nonplussed but wearily replied that they were from Kobenharven and had goods to trade. She invited the captain to inspect the cargo hold should he wish. Before he answered a short but officious looking man spoke with the lead military man in Franecian.

The militia group disappeared as quickly as they had arrived on the scene. The man in charge of the dock now addressed Elita in perfect Celta, "My Dear Captain Elita, so nice to see you again, shall we talk business?"

Elita left the dockside with the harbourmaster. Her crew prepared for the imminent unloading, as did the gangs of dock workers. It took fifteen minutes for the formalities to be signed and for Elita to grease the man's palm.

"Do you think that Matai and the rest of the Atlassia would be willing to trade some of their goods for top quality

Franecian wine?" Elita smiled at Tahira, "I know you were planning on leaving us here but I also know that you are itching to get home and now I have a damn good reason to escort you there." She bowed flamboyantly, "We would welcome your company my lady." Elita laughed, "Besides you'd only get a sore backside travelling all that way on horseback."

The smile on Tahira's face gave Elita the answer she had hoped for with the additional hug providing final confirmation.

Joining the rest of the crew they loaded their cargo onto Aija and waited patiently for the tide to take them on the next leg of their journey south towards Atlassia.

"We should be able to get you there in fourteen days with one day extra to trek to the mountains." Elita was hoping this would be in line with Tahira's expectations, which it was. Tahira had all but given up on arriving on the same day as her beloved Amir.

"Well I think we could make it in ten days." Both Elita and Tahira had a startled look on their faces as they turned to face Jasmina, "Well by my calculations if we cut across the bay here," she pointed to a map on the desk.

"Isn't that where we saw the pirates?" Tahira nodded her agreement to Elita's question.

Jasmina however ignored the comment, "Also there is another bit here." She moved her finger further south on the hand drawn image in front of them, "By moving away from the coastline we can save a lot of time."

"But if we get the direction wrong we could miss our target and end up on the other side of the world?" Elita was concerned, "And then there are the pirates."

"I don't think this is a problem, especially if we travel at night!"

Elita was now even more concerned, "No sailor in their right mind would cross the ocean at night. The risks are too great. It's one thing to travel on a cloudless night under a full moon hugging the coastline but we are heading into less well known seas. If you look at the map and we miss by just a bit we could end up literally in the middle of nowhere."

"But only if we miss." Jasmina was calm and confident, "Look, you've travelled at night before using the polestar and the land for reference." Elita nodded, "So travelling at night is possible. In what I am suggesting the only thing different is the lack of a visible coastline. However as I have shown you before I can work out how fast Aija is moving so by referencing the Polestar I can plot on the map where we are and adjust our course accordingly. If my calculations are right we should make it easily inside ten days." Jasmina's voice was calm.

Tahira watched and listened as Jasmina explained her logic to Elita. She explained in great detail her calculations. "I'll tell you what. Prove to me that it works by using it to chart the next few days sailing. If your predictions match then I will talk to the crew." Elita remained reluctant to risk her ship and crew but she had to accept that any merchant who could get their goods to market ahead of their competitors was always going to succeed. Sailing the big oceans at night would give them a major advantage, if, and it was a big if, it worked.

Elita now turned her attention back to Tahira, "My ever so friendly harbour master informs me that the Franecians are no longer dealing with the Celts. Apparently several warships left Celta last week heading for Franecia, unfortunately for them, they did not know about the shifting sandbanks and they ran aground. Those that were able tried to swim ashore at the next low tide but the few that made it were tired and easily picked off by the watchmen." She paused briefly, "It does explain why the wine was so cheap as normally they would sell the vast majority of it to the Celts."

It was at that moment they began to feel Aija being raised off the mud flats as the tide turned. With one final check to ensure that their cargo was well secured Elita issued the orders to cast off and head south. The crew welcomed the change of plan. It would be nice to be rid of the more extreme wintry forces. It was made even better when Elita explained how much profit they could expect from the resultant trade.

As they headed westwards along the coast they soon came across the watery grave of several Celta warships. They were as large as the Norseman's but again didn't stand much chance against the forces of nature. Being careful to avoid the same fate they steered into deeper water. Jasmina was updating her maps and charts all the time. She had found her role on board Aija and was not going to let it go.

They traversed the small bay where they had encountered pirates several lunar cycles before. The memories where still clear to both Elita and Tahira. Tahira especially felt the pain of condemning so many men to their early death. As a further test of Jasmina's navigational theories they made this crossing at night, which worked almost perfectly. At first light she realised that she was a couple of hundred yards away from where she expected the ship to be. She worked on the solution all day and was pleased to announce at the evening meal that she had resolved it. "I needed to take into account the effect of the tide so I have made some adjustments and we are good to go."

They kept close to the coastline for the next few days until they reached the point that they knew they had to make a decision. Elita had done this journey a few times before. She had always headed directly south to keep the coastline on the port side. She knew that after a few days the land would force them west for another several days sailing before they could resume their southerly heading. But, she knew if they headed southwest at this point they could potentially reduce the journey by almost a week but they would have a few days sailing where they could not see landfall and to make matters worse they would have to sail overnight.

The crew busied themselves onshore stocking up on provisions. They slept well that night. In the morning Elita gave them the green light to proceed southwest and into the unknown and uncharted waters of the deep sea.

The day went very well, at one point they were escorted by a pair of large whales. Astra was particularly interested in them.

At midday Jasmina suddenly realised that the position of the sun in the sky was ever so slightly higher, she needed to make adjustments which she conveyed to the helmsman. As darkness descended so did some clouds. The wind picked up. Although not dangerous it was clear that the weather affects the deeper water more than they had thought. Some of the more hardy souls were still able to sleep in their swinging hemp hammocks. The girls were not as fortunate as their bunks exaggerated the rolling of the ocean waves.

Tahira was aware that Jasmina was becoming a bit concerned. The cloud cover was so expansive that she was unable to see the polestar. She took herself away to the prow of the ship. She was looking into Astra's eyes as she imagined what the view would be like if there were fewer clouds in the sky. Astra's eyes widened as she watched her mother go into a trance like state. She also saw her mother's necklace glow. Instinctively she reached out to touch the shining crystals but they dulled very quickly as her mother made a funny face in her direction which made her giggle.

Tahira took Astra back to her cabin. The bed had stopped rocking. Without much thought Tahira imagined water boiling on top of a small fire in a clay built oven. The glow on her necklace was barely noticeable.

Elita and Jasmina soon joined them for a midnight pine tea. Jasmina was happy again as good fortune had cleared the clouds and she could see the Polestar and advise the helmsman to change direction slightly. Only Astra had seen what had happened and she wasn't telling anyone.

The next couple of days passed without incident. The weather was fine throughout. There was just enough of a breeze to keep them moving steadily forward.

"Land ahoy!" A young man who was working up high atop the mast shouted to alert the other members of the crew. He pointed towards the land and they changed course accordingly. Jasmina was slightly annoyed as they could have gone on a bit further before heading towards the coast but she had proven herself. They made landfall pretty much where she had predicted. She had saved them at least three, possibly four days of travel. Tahira too was pleased. All things being equal she should get to the city of Atlassia a day or two before Amir. She was looking forward to a hot bath.

TAHIRA THE ELEMENTAL

They pushed on and after another four days sailing they reached the river estuary. The winter rains had flushed the sand backs away. The banks of the river were brimming with greenery and the warm sun was welcomed by all. They released their anchor and tied up at the small wooden jetty.

Tahira noted how there were a few more tents and wooden structures in the village since last time she was there. They were unfortunately unable to unload their cargo as the villagers were waiting for a caravan train to arrive with their food supplies from Atlassia which was overdue.

"Be careful, all is not as it seems!"

"Are you OK Tahira?" Jasmina was concerned about her friend who had stopped speaking mid-sentence with a faraway look in her eyes.

Tahira blinked and quickly shook her head, "I can't wait any longer. I will take Astra and row one of the local canoes up the river as far as I can. I need to see Amir."

Neither Jasmina nor Elita cautioned her against it, "Well, we'll go with you, my men will know what to do when the caravan arrives, besides with a bit of luck we will get there first thing in the morning, just in time for a nice hot bath." Elita looked across at her lover, "Now that is something to look forward too!"

They arrived at the foot of the mountain path a bit later than they had hoped but still full of excitement. They began their walk. Tahira was the first to note that it was quiet, unusually quiet. There was no bird song. At this time of year the sky should be full of their chatter. The last time Tahira had walked this way she had the sense that she was being followed by multiple pairs of eyes but not today. They reached the gatehouse. The drawbridge was up but there was no one around. They carefully climbed the nearby cliff edge. They made painstakingly slow progress and would have been easy targets should there be anyone around to take advantage of their situation. Circling around the chasm in front of them they were able to peer into the city itself. There were no obvious signs of human activity although they could see some farm animals milling around in their fields.

Tahira thought she saw movement out of the corner of her eye as they started on the road up to the main square. They came across a house with the door left open. Gazing inside they could see a farmers family slumped with their heads on a kitchen table. Tahira saw the movement again. She thought she recognised that form, "Amir, Amir." She shouted but if it was him he didn't hear her. Elita and Jasmina entered the house. The people were alive, their breathing was shallow, but they couldn't rouse them.

Tahira handed Astra to Jasmina, "Hold her for me please. I need to catch up with Amir." She ran as fast as she could up the gentle slope towards the main square and Matai's house.

She entered Matai's house. Atalasian and Abidemi where slumped on the kitchen table. Matai was lying on the floor with a small bronze flagon in her hand. It looked familiar but she didn't have time to dwell on it. They were still alive but there was no sign of Amir.

Still in a state of panic she searched the nearby civic buildings but without success. She went to her schoolhouse. Her quarters had been ransacked. Through the door that led onto the school games field, she caught a glimpse of a figure moving quickly at the far end of the field next to the lookout platform that overlooked Lake Mediati. She called out as she ran. The figure turned to face her, it was Amir and he was pleased to see her.

She ran into his arms. She was breathless, "Thank the Gods that you are safe, I have missed you so much." She kissed him, "Do you know what's happened here?"

Amir was thoughtful, "I arrived last night and what you see around you is how it was to me as well. I am so glad you are here." He reached out to hold her amulet, "So pretty, and even nicer with the new yellow stone!" He let it go and placed his hands on her shoulders and turned her around to face Lake Mediati. "Look at this wondrous sight."

From her cliff top vantage point she could see scores of battleships, "They look like Persean ships. Sadiri had said that they had dismantled their navy..." The pain in her back was intense, she fell to her knees. Amir's dagger had grazed her heart. She coughed as a little blood entered her throat.

Amir grabbed her head and forcibly turned her face to meet his. He reached down and snatched the multi coloured crystal necklace. "My dear Tahira," he snarled venomously, "so young, so pretty, so misguided. Did you really think that a Persean like me would ever want to be with a pathetic Celt like you?" He spat these words out victoriously, "I remember seeing you for the first time on Aija. I watched you use your amulet to sink a pirate ship. A little while later you somehow managed to defeat the whole of the Dogon army and I noticed a new stone appear in your little necklace. Many times when you were sleeping in my arms I reached out to hold it. It felt warm to my touch and I knew it was your source of power. When I met Makida, and after I slept with her, I told her of my suspicions. We concocted a plan to see if we could destroy our mortal enemy the Mycenean King Olenus and you my little darling played your part perfectly. I had intended to kill you then but it suited my purpose for you to disappear for some time, whilst I went back and married Makida. It gave us time to prepare our military and hatch our plan. It was simple really all I had to do was to get here ahead of you with my special wine flagons with my now perfected sleeping draft and wait for you to bring me your amulet of power." He laughed, "So predictable. So pathetic." He threw her to the ground, "And now my great navy has arrived to take over the city of Atlassia. My Queen will soon join me as I sit on the throne once beloved of the useless and weak King Atalasian." He raised his arms triumphantly as a signal to the Persean ships below, and with Tahira's amulet in his hands he ran towards the city gate leaving Tahira to her slow and painful death.

Jasmina was the first to arrive at Tahira's side, closely followed by Elita. They couldn't get a pulse. Astra, who Jasmina had placed on the ground as they tried to revive Tahira, was smiling. Elita and Jasmina stood up and tried to comfort each other. Their friend was lost, betrayed by the man she loved.

"Mama." Astra's voice was clear as she placed her right hand on her mother's lifeless body. Her unexpected voice shocked Elita and Jasmina into silence. They looked intently at Astra, no baby should be able to speak at this stage of their life, not even a magical one, but here she was. A still smiling Astra ignored their look of surprise before repeating her call to her mother before she closed her eyes. With tears streaming down their faces, Elita and Jasmina fell to their knees and watched.

TAHIRA THE ELEMENTAL

Tahira was angry. Angry at Amir yes but angry at herself. She replayed in her mind all of the experiences she had shared with Amir, all the conversations, all of his words. How had she been so naïve? Why hadn't she seen the truth? She had blinded herself with love for a man who had played her like the child she was. And now, through his betrayal, she had paid the ultimate price. She had dared to believe in his love and respect for her as an equal but... The pain inside her grew.

"*Mama.*" Tahira felt rather than heard the word but how could she, and whose voice was it? In her mind's eye she saw the dark clouds that where surrounding her dissipate and clear. She was in a shadow space with nothing below or above. There was an ethereal image of a young woman, she was familiar to her.

"*Astra, is that you?*" Her words were projected from her mind and not spoken. Tahira was now hit with a massive wave of grief. Her love for Astra was total and she would never feel that love again. The image in front of her smiled.

"*My dear Tahira.*" It was her inner voice this time but it was being projected from another ghostly entity standing on her left side. The image was of a beautiful young woman. A face unknown to her but somehow she knew who it was.

"*Mother.*" It wasn't a question. Tahira felt her mother's love and smiled.

Siria held out her hands. Both Tahira and Astra did the same. As they joined hands together to complete the circle Tahira felt a surge of energy rise through her.

"*Be at peace my darling daughter. You have work to do, it is your destiny.*"

Tahira's life passed by her eyes in a flash. The images focused on man's lust for power and greed. She saw wars, death and destruction. She saw a land scorched, devoid of life. She knew what she had to do.

"*But I can't, what about the innocents?*" A picture of a smiling Morgana came to the fore. "*I have killed so many people already.*"

"*Some will survive but if you don't do what must be done then no one will survive. That's why I couldn't warn you about Amir, you had to learn for yourself. Know this my child. This planet is dying, abused by the greed of man. It's destruction assured by humanity's lust for power. The people of this planet need to change their ways and that change starts with you. The people of Atlassia need you, the Earth needs you.*"

"*But I can't, he took my amulet.*"

"*You don't need a trinket. You are an elemental, a child of the stars. You need to let the materialistic things go. Free your mind and let your spirit loose. Release your emotions and know your truth. Know who you really are, Tahira, the daughter of Siria and mother of Astra. Know what must be done and fulfil your destiny.*"

Tahira saw images of Matai playing with her son and watched in horror as they crumbled into dust. Then she saw Jasmina and Elita holding hands before they too became dust. Morgana and Namud's family followed suit. She saw Sigurdsson hunched over an open book. He was crying. She felt that loss.

Her anger returned. An ember stoked by unwanted images. She brought to mind the last thing she saw when she was alive. The image was of Amir, her betrayer, laughing at her. Her anger became rage. It was blinding, all consuming. She let it loose.

TAHIRA THE ELEMENTAL

Tahira, the elemental star child, drew the energy from her mother and daughter. She added it to her own. She forged it, she moulded it, she shaped it and then she released it.

She imagined storms the like of which the earth had never experienced before. They were all powerful, swirling and twisting, cyclonic tempests of doom. She saw huge trees lifted out of the ground like discarded feathers. Ships of all sizes were plucked from the oceans, lifted high into the air before being thrashed against jagged rocks, splintering into matchsticks. The violent tempests created waves a hundred feet tall that smashed into the coast, pounding rock into stone and stone into sand. The storm force gales picking up the sand and blasting it against anything in its path.

She imagined the land splitting apart creating canyons of molten magma. She saw huge volcanoes erupting and spewing their fiery lava breath into the air. These land dragons vomiting death and destruction. She envisioned hell on earth. Then she imagined the city of Atlassia rise up as an island above the tumult. She cocooned it against the might of her creation.

Then she saw the little ship Aija and its crew, she imagined lifting it up in a protective bubble as the land around it split asunder allowing the cold ocean waters to surge across the now sunken land bridge. The tsunami of salt water smashed away anything and everything that stood in its way. The old tribal lands of Atlantea were flooded in minutes but still the watery surge moved forward. It reached the ridge looking over Dogon country and poured down over it with a ferocious intensity. The water picked up the desert sand and blasted the villages into rubble, nothing remained. People ran in fear for their lives but it was to no avail. Thousands of broken, misshapen corpses bobbed up and down on the surface of the water. The twisted wreckage of flesh was barely recognisable as human.

In her mind's eye Tahira saw the sea now rush to the north of the island of Atlassia. The power of the ocean water mixed with the turbulent Lake Mediati. A giant, powerful tidal wave pushed forward sweeping everything in its path away. She imagined the monstrous tsunami devastate all of the coastal towns and cities. The Mycenean city of Zakros and the Persean city of Susa paid the ultimate price. Even the magnificent stone buildings where swept away like toy wooden blocks, crumbled ruins visible only to fish.

In her mind's eye she saw the broken bodies of countless mariners and militia men washed up on ever rising shorelines. They displayed a disturbing rhythm of movement, a macabre dance of broken human puppets. She watched the futile attempt of thousands of people as they tried to outrun the maelstrom that she had created.

The rage that had consumed and controlled her began to ease and Tahira began to draw herself back, the storm had gone. The explosive venting of magma was replaced with the hiss of superheated water, but even this receded as Tahira brought her mind's vision back towards Atlassia. She released it from its cocoon before removing the protective blanket that she had placed around Aija. The waves where placated, her rage was over.

Then she saw him. Amir's lifeless and shredded body lay at the foot of the northern entrance gate. His still open eyes were haunted, even demonic. She was overcome with pity as she watched the sea take, what was left of her former love, back down to its final watery resting place.

Then came the over whelming sense of guilt. What about the hundreds and thousands of innocent lives that had been lost?

"It had to be done, the earth needed to be reborn, you are its Mother, its guardian and protector. Humanity had lost its way."

Tahira had a vision of the future. She saw a picture of endless wars with men constantly fighting one another for the rest of time. She saw empires rise and fall. Countless millions of lives lost to service the greed of the few. Many of them unwilling, some misguided but all of them wasted. She reluctantly accepted that her actions were justified but...

Back in her shadowy realm Tahira released the hands that held her. She dropped to her knees crying in despair. Her tears felt real, she saw it fall as rain across the whole land.

"And now my beloved granddaughter you have one more thing to do."

With a smile the ethereal image of a young woman moved to comfort her mother.

Epilogue

"Mama."

Tahira felt the words rather than heard them. She opened her eyes. She was lying in her own bed, in her quarters at the schoolhouse. As she moved to sit herself upright she heard a cry of joy.

Matai rushed to her side and hugged her. Jasmina and Elita took their turn desperately trying to contain their excitement. Astra looked up from the crib she was sharing with Abidemi. She smiled before yawning and settling back down to take her afternoon nap.

"I don't know what or how but we are so happy to see you. We thought that bastard had killed you." Elita cried tears of joy.

"How long have I been away?" Tahira was clearly still weak but managed to sit herself up in her bed, "And thank you for tidying up my house." She gratefully accepted the cup of hot pine tea that Jasmina offered her.

"In total it has been forty days and forty nights." Matai offered, "Which is a lot longer than the two days we were knocked out for. I can't believe that we trusted him. We were so pleased to see him and he seemed genuinely happy to be here. He brought us all flagons of sweet wine and insisted that we toast your forthcoming arrival." She shook her head, "What a monster, he would have enslaved us all or worse had us killed." She began shaking with rage when she thought of Atalasian and Abidemi.

"Well he's gone now and you are all safe."

"Yes, thanks to you." Matai paused thoughtfully, "More importantly, how are you?" She didn't need to finish her question, Tahira knew her well enough to know what she was intimating.

"Look, the sun, at long last the sun is shining." Jasmina threw back the drapes from the window and the sunlight flooded the room with its golden glow, "Come Elita we must let the people know that their teacher is alive and well."

After the two of them departed Matai once more addressed Tahira, "Apparently the rain started after those two lovebirds found you sprawled across the floor at the old viewpoint," Matai laughed, "and it hasn't stopped until you opened your eyes a moment ago. That's a strange coincidence, don't you think?" She paused briefly, "They tell me that Astra twice called out 'Mama' as she lay next to you. Although she has not spoken since so we think they might have imagined it. Anyway, they brought you back here as they didn't know what to do. They were convinced you were dead and in fact they placed a veil over your face. Jasmina fed Astra who kept smiling. They left you here overnight and when they came back with Astra in the morning you were breathing normally but they could not wake you. A miracle is what they called it. The rest of Atlassia began waking up throughout the rest of the day. I told them that you would be alright and that you just needed to rest." She hugged her friend, "It's so good to see you."

Tahira smiled at her friend, "It's good to see you again Matai. And I really like those wisps of grey in your hair, it's very, becoming." Then she laughed, "You should close your mouth you know, it's not very lady like."

Matai joined in the laughter.

TAHIRA THE ELEMENTAL

Tahira felt well enough to take a stroll. Matai willingly offered her arm for support as Astra and Abidemi were sleeping soundly. Tahira walked with her friend to the northern view point. All they could see was a vast ocean stretching out from the base of the cliffs as far as the eye could see.

"It's a bit different from the old lake that used to be there." offered Matai, "It is the same in the south. All our old lands are gone and are under water. We are now an island. All our ships have gone. Only Aija remains and Elita has taken her out a couple of times. There is some coastline to the north that she recognises although Jasmina mentioned that the cliffs used to be much higher than they are now. Now that they know you are OK they will shortly leave for Kobenharven. Elita informs me that her mother was going to stay with friends in the northern mountains of Agathyria. She is obviously worried about her family."

"I know." whispered Tahira, "She has lost so much." She paused recoiling at the horror of her memory, "I have killed so many people Matai, more than it is possible to count. I don't deserve to live." Tahira wept uncontrollably.

Matai held her friend for several minutes waiting for the tears to subside, "If anyone deserves to live it is you Tahira. You did what you did out of love, out of love for Astra and your friends. If Amir hadn't tried to kill you and enslave us then maybe you wouldn't have done what you did. But there would have been others. People see what Atalasian and his people have achieved and they are envious. Humanity's lust for power is never ending. Elita has told us about other kingdoms hell bent on war with their neighbours. Man needs to take this opportunity of rebirth that you have given them. Yes the price was high but I for one would be willing to pay that price and I would do what you did if I had the power to do so. In a single moment you have given us the greatest gift that any of us can have and that is hope, without it we are truly lost."

Matai wiped away Tahira's tears. She laughed, "Hey, I wonder what old Koranda would say if he could see us now?"

They walked back to the house to be greeted by Jasmina. She excitedly held out her hand and offered Tahira her amulet. "One of the guards found it this morning at the gate, he fixed the chain."

Tahira grinned and asked Jasmina to pass on her gratitude. She turned to the crib and placed it in the hand of Astra who was still sleeping soundly next to Abidemi.

• • • •

"Mama. Mama. They're coming, I can see their ship." Seren was shouting excitedly as she ran down from the northern viewing point to her house. Her long blonde hair flowed gracefully behind her as she ran. Tahira looked out of the window at her beautiful blue eyed daughter. Seren jumped into her mother's arms.

"Will you go and fetch your sister please? She's at Jasmina and Elita's house helping them get ready. I'll meet you both at the library."

Tahira wasted no time in getting to the great library of Atlassia. "Sigu. Their ship is just about to dock."

Sigurdsson looked up from his book and into the eyes of the woman he adored more than life itself. Standing up he reached out to hold her.

"Yuk." Seren teased as she arrived with Astra who smiled.

TAHIRA THE ELEMENTAL

"Shall we?" Astra took hold of her mother's hand. She would shortly celebrate her eleventh birthday but there was a maturity that belied her youthful appearance. With Sigurdsson holding his wife of nine years in one hand and his eight year old daughter in the other, the family of four made their way down to the northern harbour of the great city of Atlassia.

King Atalasian, Queen Matai and their son Abidemi had just stepped off their royal ship. They exchanged hugs.

"How was the trip Atalasian? I bet you are glad to be home after such a long voyage?" Sigurdsson offered to carry the King's bags for him.

"Yes I am pleased to be home," King Atalasian took a deep breath, "It was however a very successful trip. We have signed several peace treaties along with various trade agreements. You will also be please to know my friend that I have brought you several cases of books for your library. There is enough there to keep you busy for years." He clapped Sigurdsson on his shoulder.

"Did you bring our special guests?" Tahira asked Matai.

Matai smiled, she didn't need to answer. "Tahira, oh my goodness, is that really you? You look amazing." Morgana dropped her bags and rushed to hug her old friend.

"Hello Morgana." Astra stood beside her mother.

"It can't be." With tears in her eyes Morgana looked into a pair of eyes she had not seen in many years, "Astra. You are as beautiful as your mother. You won't remember me but the last time I saw you, you were but a baby and I used to hold you. You used to give the best cuddles."

As Astra held out her arms to hug Morgana, she whispered, "But I do remember Morgana, I remember it all." Morgana swept her up without any intention of ever letting her go.

Namud, Nawali and her partner Zirak had also arrived on the boat along with several other members of Namud's family who Tahira had not seen in a decade.

"So she doesn't know then?" Nawali was now talking to Tahira as the rest of the entourage began to make their way up to main part of the city.

"No although it might be a bit difficult to keep it quiet now. As you can tell the people of Atlassia love their King and Queen and Elita is bound to hear the commotion." Tahira paused and pointed to a small guest house near the school, "You and Zirak are staying here."

Tahira looked behind her to see Astra, who had now wriggled free from Morgana's clutches, leading her and the rest of the Namud clan to a large stone building normally reserved for visiting dignitaries.

Sigurdsson had offered to show Zirak around his beloved library. It was an offer he couldn't refuse.

As Tahira and Nawali arrived at the guest accommodation they heard a shout.

"Mother, what are you doing here?" Elita came running along the road with Jasmina hot on her heels.

"Hello dear. Nice to see you too." Nawali had a hint of sarcasm in her voice as Elita embraced her. "Well I wasn't going to miss my daughter's wedding now was I?"

"But who told you. We chose to get married here to keep it quiet." Elita looked at her mother who nodded in Jasmina's direction.

Jasmina looked sheepish, "I wanted your mother to share our special day, and I know that you do too so..."

Nawali interrupted, "As I have told you before I have known that marrying a man is not for you, and to be honest I don't care. The only thing that matters to me is your happiness. I love Jasmina as if she was my daughter and I am so pleased that she wants to be part of our family." she paused briefly, "I see the love you two have for each other and I want to celebrate that. I want to shout it from the roof tops for I am proud of you, my darling daughter." She did her best to hold back her tears, "Besides, you should take a leaf of Jasmina's book and write to me occasionally. I might not be able to read but Zirak can."

The celebrations began in earnest the next morning. Elita and Jasmina had wanted a quiet wedding but King Atalasian and Queen Matai were not going to let that happen.

Atalasian had always acknowledged the past. But he couldn't live in it. Every day represented a new challenge and a new opportunity for him and his people to grow. The last ten years had seen the Atlantean people make great strides across multiple subjects including science, art and philosophy. Aided and abetted by people from other lands who shared their vision. The dissemination of their views and their history only added to the development of the Atlantean society as a whole. It was helped in no small part by what had happened a decade ago. The old warring empires had been decimated overnight. Rightly or wrongly the remaining kingdoms believed that Atlassia wielded immeasurable power and that it was better for them to be an ally rather than an enemy. The Atlanteans had also mastered the sea, thanks to the seafaring skills of Elita and especially the invention of the science of navigation instigated by Jasmina. They had created trade routes and discovered lands that other countries didn't even know existed. The marriage of Elita and Jasmina was an opportunity to celebrate not just their love for each other but also the love of their family and friends for them.

Astra escorted both Elita and Jasmina to the main civic building in the centre of Atlassia city. Matai had agreed to be the celebrant and as they entered the building they were greeted with cheers, and tears, of joy from the large crowd. The whole city had welcomed the opportunity to join in the celebrations.

The rest of the day was filled with music, laughter, drinking and eating. As night fell and the feasting drew to a close, Tahira's family headed home. A tired Seren was carried by her father whilst Astra held her mother's hand.

They stopped at their door and stared into the night sky. They nodded and the brightest star appeared to shine just that little bit brighter. "Oh I meant to tell you girls," Tahira said, "For their honeymoon, Elita and Jasmina, are going to find Antarti and the dinosauri and have invited us along for the journey. That's if anyone wants to go of course?" Seren squealed in delight as Sigu knew she would. Tahira and her husband had been planning this trip for months and had waited until after the wedding to share the news with their girls. It was to be a great family adventure. Astra smiled.

· · · ·

The End

TAHIRA THE ELEMENTAL

Page

Don't miss out!

Visit the website below and you can sign up to receive emails whenever Derek M Cartwright publishes a new book. There's no charge and no obligation.

https://books2read.com/r/B-A-OYOBC-VVGBF

BOOKS 2 READ

Connecting independent readers to independent writers.

About the Author

I have had a lifelong passion for all things 'Book' related. I remember going to my local library where I grew up in Liverpool and handing my card over to the librarian as I took out various storybooks. That love of escapism I found in those stories has never left me.

As I entered the seventh decade of my lifeI finally decided that I should follow my dream and actually write a novel. Tahira The Elemental is the result. And now that the floodgates are open there are many more to follow!

Read more at https://www.derekmcartwright.com.

Milton Keynes UK
Ingram Content Group UK Ltd.
UKHW021101181124
451360UK00015B/1215